My Back Pages

O'Brien Browne

BLACK ROSE writing™

First printing

This is a work of fiction. Names, characters, businesses, places, events and incidents are either the products of the author's imagination or used in a fictitious manner. Any resemblance to actual persons, living or dead, or actual events is purely coincidental.

ISBN: 978-1-61296-457-7

PUBLISHED BY BLACK ROSE WRITING

www.blackrosewriting.com

Printed in the United States of America

Suggested retail price $15.95

My Back Pages is printed in Adobe Caslon Pro

For my family: future, present and past — in life, spirit, and memory.

My Back Pages

Ah, but I was so much older then / I'm younger than that now.

~ Bob Dylan, *My Back Pages*

1

Before it was daylight, in the deep still of the black early morning when one minute takes ten to tick off the clock, I lay securely flat on my back in bed, blinking up at the soft, formless ceiling, scratching my nose, and trying to block out the hard skeleton finger that was tapping against something metallic inside the clock, making a loud *klack-klack klack-klack* noise. I was listening beyond that, my ears pricked and tuned to a fine pitch, stomach empty and longing. The whole house was very still and quiet, except for the occasional creak and groan of settling wood, and no sound came from Kathy's or the Monster's room, nor from my parents' either. Outside my window was impenetrable, depthless blackness.

Some time earlier I had been dreaming of trenches and slow crawling tanks silhouetted against a burning red sky and I closed my eyes again to return to that place but my body would not let go. It held itself tight, expectant, and there was a wanting in the waiting which would not allow me to soar off very deep or far into the night for fear of losing myself there and then miss the not missing. I was waiting. And listening.

The morning was the beginning of freedom and there were so many things I did not want to miss not missing: Mr. Friedman and his 263-page cloth bound books, Mrs. Tannen with the long yellow teeth and sour liverwurst breath and also that stupid bully Mark Burton or the Fat Kid, or Deborah Miller who had skin like day-old baloney and pale eyes and who stared at me during lunch time until I felt like barfing when I tried to eat my baloney sandwich with a thin leaf of lettuce and too much mayonnaise and no mustard on it.

And I couldn't wait to start ignoring all the bad things at home, like my dad's wild rages, Kathy's moodiness and constant fighting with my parents, the Monster's temper tantrums and my mom's dusty poetry books. All of this would be swept away by the force of what was coming.

Finally, at the very bottom of the blackness, I could see the world just starting its slow and heavy somersault. A thin streak of light gave at last a form and a finish to the night. Then I heard the summer coming. Out there, beyond the black and the gray, past the Central Californian hills which rippled across the box-frame view of my bedroom window and probably coming from Old Man Palmer's farm, the cracked, soaring call of a rooster made it official.

It was the first day of no more school.

A rush of hot, vital blood raced through my veins and started my heart pumping double time. I wanted to jump right out of bed and dash outside, but it was still too early and it would be cold and damp outside because the summer had just now started and the warm time was not yet fully here. So, wide awake, happy and brain-crowded with what-am-I-gonna-do-today thoughts, I watched the sky working itself over, the black fading into dark gray, misshapen faces and strange animals floating past as clouds shifted, dissipated and disappeared. Then a red flame burst on the horizon and flared up into orange and yellow before dissolving against a vaulted band of blue. This was what I had been waiting for.

With a swift arch of my arm, I tossed the blanket off me and in an instant was up out of bed and pulling on my jeans, a t-shirt with a sweatshirt over that, and my boots. Before heading out, I slipped my *Case* pocketknife into my pocket. Then I went out into the summer.

I sauntered across the driveway, kicking stones with the toe of my boot, heading to the little footpath on the side of the pole barn where my dad kept his trucks, welding equipment and his big blue lathe. Just as I started to pass by the barn, Duke stuck his head out from around the corner and took a sniff at me. He never seemed to sleep and you could not go anywhere without him finding you out and following.

"Hey, Duke," I said to him, patting my knee. "C'mon, boy," and he trotted up to me, red tongue dangling from his bushy, black-haired mutt's face. I scratched his head and we set off together for a short walk.

The sky was clear, golden and magnificent. Laughing bars of light and stardust rolled down from the sun and I could smell the summer everywhere. It was not the hot, dry summer yet; that would come. Nor was it the chilly, wind-saddened days of late August; that was years away. This was the start, more spring than summer, and still fresh and green and vivid. The country air was pungent with the rich scents of earth, sharp resin wafting off the chaparral and the snappy crispness of tall grass.

This was the summer of youth, my last. It was bright and cheery and simple and the long, gentle days would unfold onwards in a never-ending progression. There would be adventures in the hills, camping in the tent under a sky diamonded with stars, visits from friends and tracking rabbits and deer and quail through the bush. There would be no time left in the coming crowded weeks for books and teachers, rules and wagging fingers. Nothing could stain the galloping days, and nothing could bring me down. Of this I was quite sure. The summer would not allow it, for it was powerful, insistent, overwhelming and pure.

And it had never failed me before.

2

When Duke and I got back home it was still quite early. Duke wandered off to stick his nose into his water bowl and I entered the kitchen, a fierce hunger suddenly roaring up inside my empty belly as the smells of frying bacon and eggs, butter and toasted bread and a familiar sweetness filled my senses.

My mom, wearing an old blue robe and with a long strand of black hair hanging down over one eye, was working at the stove. At the table sat the Monster, feeding.

"Hi there, Monster," I said, going to the refrigerator and pouring myself a large glass of orange juice. "Who did your hair this morning? It looks really nice."

"Shuddup," said the Monster, whose real name was Mary Ellen. I called her Monster because her curly hair, like mine, tended to frizz and if left uncombed stood out in a huge tangled halo around her head. "Your hair doesn't look so good either, you know," she added. I stuck my tongue out at her and she retaliated with the same, as I sat down across from her.

"Would you like to eat?" asked my mom.

"Yup."

"Don't say 'yup,' say 'yes'."

"Yes."

"Pancakes, too?"

"Yu--es."

"One egg or two?"

"Two."

"'Please. '"

"Two please," I said. Even in her old blue robe my mom looked elegant. She held her chin tilted up, placed her feet at angles like a ballerina and her butterfly hands glided through the air, gracefully sprinkling salt and pepper on the popping eggs.

"Where was you--" began Mary Ellen.

"'Were you,'" corrected my mom.

"--were you all mornin' long?"

"Just out messin' around with Duke."

"I wanna go to the pond today."

"I don't."

"Take me, Del, I wanna go to the pond." The Monster's little round face was reddening.

"It's too dangerous for you. You'll fall in and drown yourself."

"Mom! I wanna go, I wanna go!" Bright crimson burned her pinched face and her wild hair shook with rage.

"Take your sister down to the pond later, OK Del?"

"Aw mom," I said looking up at my mom as she brought my plate to me. There was something in her airy movements, her kind mouth, a warm something in her eyes and voice that was irresistible. "OK, Monster," I said to my little sister, "we'll go down later on."

"Yeah!" said Mary Ellen, scooping some scrambled eggs onto her fork.

I shook a couple of drops of hot sauce on my eggs, tore off a piece of bread and dipped its jagged crusty edge into the golden yolk. Then Kathy came into the kitchen from her room. She was wearing tight new jeans, white boots and a nice looking blouse, and her hair was combed.

"My, you look like something this morning," said my mom. "You've got plans?"

"I'm goin' down with Shelly and Peggy to Atascadero Lake."

"Why don't you take Mary Ellen with you?" I suggested.

Kathy's eyes burned hotly at me. "Fat chance." Spinning around, she opened the refrigerator door, bent down and came up again with a carrot in her mouth.

"Aren't you at least going to eat a real breakfast?" my mom asked.

"No time. I got to get ready," said Kathy, carrot waggling between her hurried words.

"Well, how are you going to get to the lake?"

Kathy bit off a big chunk of orangeness and said something.

"What?" asked my mom.

Kathy swallowed and took another bite. "Ernie's takin' me, us."

"I see."

"He's pickin' me up at the bottom of our road."

"Ernie Porter, you mean?"

"Yeah. Bye," said Kathy, moving quickly to the door.

"Wait a sec," said my mom, putting the egg spatula down on the kitchen counter. "What time will you guys be back?"

"Late."

"How late?"

"Tenish?"

"Be in by nine o'clock. You know how your father is."

"Bye." The screen door slammed shut and Kathy was gone.

My mom put the frying pan in the sink, then opened a cupboard, took out a mug and filled it with coffee. Cupping the mug with both hands, she leaned against the counter, bending slightly forward over the hot coffee, letting thin lines of steam snake up around her face. After a minute she said, "Del, what do you think of that Porter boy?"

"Which one?"

"Ernie."

I shrugged. "I dunno. Seems like a nice guy, I guess."

"Does he smoke?"

I shrugged again.

"Is he a safe driver?"

"Dunno. Never seen him drive before."

"What's his father do?"

"Beats me, mom. I just met him a couple of times. Why all the questions?" I looked at my mom, who was looking out the window at the dirt road which ran downhill from our house and turned into another dirt road which led you to yet another one that brought you

12

finally to Highway 41.

This time my mom shrugged. "Oh, just wondering..." and her voice trailed off.

I ate the rest of my eggs and toast and bacon, and a couple of pancakes with a dollop of creamy butter on top. There was not so much I could tell my mom about Ernie except that he was big like a grown-up only instead of a suit he wore jeans and old tie-dyed t-shirts and an Army surplus jacket and he had long, shaggy brown hair and big hands with hair on the backs of them and his eyebrows grew in a long unbroken line across his face and sometimes he scared me. He and my sister sometimes kissed and they had secrets and whispered things to each other and then looked up at me and laughed and one time when my parents were out Ernie came over and we were all in the living room, watching *Laugh In* on the TV and I was sitting on the floor, the Monster lying next to me, asleep, and Kathy sat on the sofa, kissing Ernie and not even watching *Laugh In*, just kissing Ernie. I wasn't looking at them or anything but I knew they were kissing because of the wet smacking and from the sides of my eyes I caught a glimpse of Ernie's big hairy hand going up my sister's skirt and she was letting him do it. So I kept my head stiff and aimed at the TV, not wanting to look, but hearing the kissing noises and low whispering and I knew that Ernie's hand was between my sister's legs without having to actually see it. I didn't know exactly what was going on, but that looked awfully like a boy-girl thing and I was not going to tell my mom anything about that. It was embarrassing. She could ask Kathy herself.

After breakfast, I went into my room and lay on the bed, flicking through a *Sgt. Rock* comic book. But I'd read this one a hundred times before and got bored with it and threw it on the floor. Then I crawled across the bed and dropped down into a large orange beanbag. It felt cold and clammy on my skin and squeaked when my body settled down into it. I leaned back very far and hung my head over the edge of the bag, looking at the world turned upside down. From the ceiling-floor hung a *Nieuport 17* and a *Fokker* with three wings and an *S.E. 5a*, all model airplanes I had built and painted myself and then strung from the ceiling with fishing line. On one wall was a black and white

13

photo of the Beatles, clipped from *Look* magazine and a bookcase filled with novels and history books and in the corner a brown and gold trash can. Stuck above that was a black and white picture of Robert F. Kennedy cut out of *Life* magazine. I looked at the door and out the window at the sky beneath me, then back into the room again to another corner in which my BB gun rested, its barrel pointing upwards. I let my mouth hang open and I felt the blood trickling into my head, making my eyes bulge and the skin tingle and throb. Suddenly, I sat up and the room spun and wobbled and my head felt light and heavy at the same time. I did this a couple of times until my neck began to hurt, so I rolled out of the bean bag and crawled across the floor to pick up a shoe box filled with tiny men and horses, all painted by me. Then I went outside, leaving the house quietly because if my mom saw me with nothing to do, she would have made me pull weeds in the garden.

Stepping outside, my eyes narrowed because of the bright sunshine. Cloudless and unlimited, the sky formed a pure painted backdrop to the surrounding hills thickly covered with bushy chaparral. From overhead came a distant cry and looking up I saw a hawk gliding into the sun.

I walked out near the pole barn again where there was a sand heap. Dropping down on my knees, I carefully picked out the Cheyenne warriors and U.S. Cavalry men from the shoe box and set them an arm's length away in two piles so that my hands could get to work sculpting the towering canyons and deep ravines of Wyoming from the sand, then a wooden frontier fortress for General Custer and his men. The Bighorn Mountains sprang up to the left of this where the Cheyenne and Arapaho and Lakota lived in tepees near a lake in a forest filled with grizzly bears and mountain lions. After a couple of days, the troops issued out of the fort, riding double-file towards the mountains, stupid General Custer completely unaware of where he was leading his men, while the Indians gathered carefully and silently together, watchful, letting the cavalry men move deeper into the ravine with high stone walls and a narrow path leading down to the plains below. At last Chief Dull Knife raised and dropped his arm and the warriors dashed down from their hiding places in the crags and unleashed a deadly volley of gravel that toppled the surprised white men from their horses. Custer was the first to get it. Most of the others were wiped out before they could regroup and return fire. It was a fierce battle that raged for several minutes. After that the men changed into Robin Hood and knights in armor, then to spike-helmeted Germans from the First World War, then back to Indians and cavalry again. With a grand sweep of my hand, mountains fell and reemerged as vast plains. Castles crumbled into rivers which rose up again into cities and greened into the forests of North Dakota. I was a hundred different men. A general now, or a chief or a silver knight or a grizzled, cigar-smoking sergeant, I rallied my men, fought desperately and tragically, fell nobly or yelled when victory was in sight. In a loudly whispered voice I whinnied like a horse, whistled and ricocheted like bullets, *chinged* like swords and puffed out my cheeks to make the booming, demented explosions of artillery shells.

"Whatcha doin'?"

Startled, I looked up. "Nuthin'," I said to the Monster, my voice suddenly my own again. I could feel my face beginning to burn.

"You're playin', aren'tcha?"

"No. Go away."

"Are too. Daddy says you're too old to play."

"So?" My voice was stronger now and I tried to use it to intimidate.

"So I'm tellin'."

"Good. Go tell and see if I care."

"I'm tellin' daddy when he gets home."

"I don't care," I said, turning back to my soldiers, "go ahead and tell like a baby."

"I'm not a baby."

"Baby, baby, baby."

"Shuddup!" said the Monster, her face folding in on itself and her lower lip starting to tremble.

"You shuddup and stop tellin' on people all the time like a cry baby."

"I'm not a baby," she protested, stamping one bare foot.

"OK, OK," I said, wishing now to end this. "What are you doin' out here anyways?"

15

"You promised to take me to the pond." Mary Ellen was creepy that way. She remembered everything. "You promised."

One look into that face, sometimes fat and simple like an infant's, other times with a wise, knowing look in it that did not fit at all with her years, told me I was not going to get out of this one. I stood up, brushed sand from my knees and off the seat of my pants, then extended both arms. "Oh c'mon," I said, "I'll carry you. You can't walk out there barefoot."

Duke materialized from the air and accompanied us as we strolled down to the pond, and from the bushes Taffy suddenly appeared. She was a small brown and black dog, with beady eyes and a way of keeping her head down low and her shoulders hunched like she was used to being beaten, which she never was. Sullen and moody, she only hung around our family because that was where she could get an easy meal. Mary Ellen said, "Hi Taffy," but she did not even look up. Then Mary Ellen said, "Taffy looks funny. Her belly's not right."

I cocked my head and looked sideways at the dog. "You're right. Her stomach's bigger, like its bloated or somethin'. Maybe she's sick or got worms. That's why lately she's been acting weirder than usual."

The pond lay well beyond the pole barn. With Mary Ellen in my arms and Duke at my side, I walked over the rocky earth, bordered on both sides by hills covered in blue-green chaparral, heading towards a small swelling of earth, behind which came the music of a hundred baritones, singing lustily into the summer's morning air. We clambered up the hump and, clutching Mary Ellen tightly to my chest, I slid down its rocky slope, the rocks underneath my feet chattering loudly and rolling away from me to stop just at the lip of the pond. The singing cut off abruptly, making the air seem suddenly empty and sad.

I set Mary Ellen down and motioned for her to keep quiet. Crouching, we crept up to the water's edge and squatted down, keeping ourselves still so that the music would start up again. While waiting, I noticed how low the water had dropped because of the lack of rain. A light green line was scribbled a few feet up the bank, dried-out moss marking the water's high point from last winter; by mid-summer the pond would be completely dried up. I examined the water. It was dark green and covered by thin, mushy algae and smelled like boiled eggs. Flies droned lazily over its surface and fragile, almost transparent insects with long spidery legs skated delicately across the water where there was no algae covering. All around the pond grew chaparral, coming right down to the water.

Suddenly I heard a soft plop and my eyes darted over to where it had come from. The Monster was pointing to where slow water rings spread out from a vanished epicenter. I kept very still and scanned the surface of the pond carefully. Luckily, Duke and Taffy had scampered off into the bush, which greatly improved my hunting chances.

There was another plop and after that a loud croak broke out into the morning's crispness. This was answered by another, a bit further away, and then another until the choir was in full swing again. I watched intently, finally picking out a blob of green that was of a darker shade than the surrounding algae. A hole opened up in the dark green and a croak came out. Slowly I reached down and covered a half-cupped hand over the tiny blob. Noiselessly, the frog sprang upwards and I closed my hand around it.

Fingers curling in firmly--but not too tightly--I pulled the frog to me and made a bowl with two hands. The frog was extremely tiny, squatting with a benign expression on his face on lithe rubber legs. His little pads splayed themselves out and he shifted slightly on my palm; my skin could just barely register the delicate squishiness of his body. I showed him to the Monster, who smiled, extended a finger and stroked the frog's back. After a couple minutes more of observation, I lowered my hand to the water and with a jump the frog disappeared into the murkiness.

Standing up, I looked at Mary Ellen. "Hey," I said, "I know what let's do."

"What?"

"Let's go look for rabbits. They usually hang out right around here."

"Yeah," said Mary Ellen, reaching up to me with both arms. "But you gotta carry me."

"Up you go," I said, lifting her.

Then I hollered for Duke and he came bounding out of the bush, eyes twinkling. We skirted the edge of the pond for a bit and then

Duke led us uphill, following a deer trail. Now we were in the chaparral's dark green, scratchy, bristling stiffness. All at once Duke stopped dead in his tracks, head lowered, back rigid and his nose twitching. I halted too and held my breath, following his gaze into the thick undergrowth, seeing only green and beyond that a formless black. Duke, his body stiff and trembling, took tiny, nervous steps towards something and then sprang forward, running full-out. There was a tremendous *flub-flub-flubbing* noise and a cloud of bluish-gray screamed out of the earth and exploded in a mad flapping and shrieking mass of panic into the sun. The quail rose and vanished in the sky. Instantly, all was quiet again.

"Wow wee!" said Mary Ellen, her mouth open.

We hunted for cottontails for about an hour, finding nothing but a few lizards and a field mouse. By then the first day of my freedom was beginning to darken. The sky, still wonderful, was now a deep, lapis lazuli blue. The green of the chaparral was darker and more mysterious and the earth's brown was rich and full. A breeze was blowing and in it you could smell that the day had changed itself and that the fading time was coming near. I carried Mary Ellen in my arms as she yawned and nestled her tiny little face into my neck, warm moist breath on my skin. She felt heavy and shapeless in my arms. Duke trotted alongside me, ears pricked and alert, head flicking this way and that as he picked up every warm vibration thrown off from a hidden mouse or rabbit scurrying through the undergrowth. Taffy slouched on ahead, occasionally twisting her head to look back at Duke, not us. Watching her, I noticed again how odd and distended her stomach seemed.

Arriving home, we entered the kitchen where it was warm and good smelling. The table was set for dinner, but my mom was not there. I carried Mary Ellen into her bedroom and laid her down on her bed, asleep. Then I went out to the living room where I found my mom sitting up on the couch, her head bowed into a book, and meditatively biting on a thumbnail.

"Hi," I said, entering and taking a seat in the big arm chair.

My mom slowly looked up at me, and for an instant I had the feeling that she was emerging from some place many miles away. She was wearing her reading glasses and they gave her face a different,

18

more serious look. "You're back from the wars, I see." Now she was the same old mom again.

"Yup," I said, "and I put Mary Ellen to bed. She's pooped."

"'Yes.' I'll have to wake her up then," said my mom, closing her book and removing her glasses. "She's got to eat something or she'll wake up in the middle of the night."

"I'm hungry, too. What's for dinner?"

"Quiche."

"What's that?" I asked mistrustfully, screwing up my face. My mom was always cooking weird foreign foods with funny sounding names.

"It's a French cheese pie with bacon. You'll like it."

"Well, if it's got cheese and bacon in it, I guess it'll be alright."

She glanced at her wrist. "Turn on the TV, Del," she asked me, "I'd like to catch the news. And don't jump--"

My mom was too late--I had already leapt from the chair, landing with a *thumpf* right in front of the TV. Switching it on, I hopped on one leg back to the big chair, and rolled up into it, hugging a large cushion against my stomach.

First there was the usual news about the endless war and reports on how many they had killed and how many more we had killed, and some silver-haired general with a Hollywood chin was speaking to a reporter in khaki and a floppy hat. Then I sat up in the chair, pointing at the screen and said, "Hey, it's Bobby!"

"*Shhhh*," said my mom, leaning towards the TV. Her eyes had a liquid, dreamy look in them that they usually had when she was reading a biography of some famous dead English poet.

Enthralled, I watched RFK on the TV, dressed in a gray suit with a white shirt and a thin black tie. I liked him because he was youthful and his hair was longish and his voice was high and reedy, a little like Porky Pig's and he had a funny accent. But also, there was a wistful, sad look in his eyes, and a sad quality in his face and his hunched shoulders that reminded me of winter. It made you sort of feel sorry for him and close to him at the same time. Then the screen blinked and he was gone.

My mom sighed and stood up to switch the TV off.

"You gonna vote for 'im, mom?"

"Yes, of course."

"Did you vote for his brother, too?"

My mom's eyes still had that moistness in them. "Yes, I did."

"Whodaya like better, RFK or JFK?"

"I like Bobby very much, but his brother was very special and I liked him, too. I can't say if I prefer one to the other."

"Were you sad when he got killed?"

"Yes," said my mom, putting her hand to her throat. "It was a terrible, terrible time. I cried for a week."

"Really? You cried, mom?"

"A terrible time, Del. Be glad you were too young to experience it." My mom looked at her wrist again. "It's late. Come on now, Del, let's go eat before your father gets home."

I followed my mom into the kitchen. "Why do we always gotta eat before dad comes home? TV families always eat together."

My mom handed me a large pottery salad bowl and I carried it to the table. "First of all, we're not a TV family. Secondly, you know how tired your father is when he comes home. He's got a hard job and he needs time to relax." My mom said this as she placed the cheese-bacon pie on the table and sank a knife into it.

"I guess we get on his nerves."

My mom's eyes flashed at me. "You don't get on his nerves. He loves his children, but he's just exhausted when he comes home. Here--take some salad. I'll go get Mary Ellen."

I served myself some salad. It was filled with tomatoes from our garden, radishes, celery and alfalfa sprouts and thin rings of purple onion. The olive oil glistened on the lettuce leaves; the smell of garlic was strong. I took a wedge of cheese pie, too.

"Hey, sleepy head," I said as Mary Ellen came into kitchen, rubbing an eye. Her face was red and puffy and a sweaty impression of a blanket pattern was stamped onto one side of her head. Ignoring me, she sat down.

"How's the pie?" asked my mom.

"Pretty good. What's it called again?"

"Quiche."

"*Eeeweu.* I'm not eating it," Mary Ellen said.

"It's a cheese pie, blockhead," I said.

"Mom, do I hafta eat it?"

"Why don't you at least try it, baby?"

"I don't wanna. It looks funny." The Monster was tightening her face, ready to squeeze out a tear to support her argument.

"Well," said my mom, "you don't have to if you don't want to. Eat some salad, then."

"Great, that means there'll be more for me." My eyes twinkled at my mother and she half-smiled at me.

"I wanna small piece to try," said Mary Ellen immediately. My mom put a small triangle of pie on her plate and, after a sniff, she took a bite, chewing slowly and not blinking. There were not any apparent side effects.

"Know what mom? When we were at the pond Taffy came along and I think she's sick or somethin'."

"Yeah," said Mary Ellen, speaking through mashed cheese and egg and bacon bits, "she's gotta fat tummy."

"Maybe it's worms," I said.

"She's not sick," said my mom, "your father thinks she's pregnant."

"Pregnant? Wow!"

"What's that?" asked Mary Ellen, a yellow piece of goo flying out with her question.

"Close your mouth when you chew, Mary Ellen; we all know what you're eating. Pregnant means she's carrying babies in her stomach and when they come out we'll have puppies."

"Oh boy!" cried Mary Ellen. "Puppies!"

At that moment, Duke and Taffy began barking outside and there was a loud, familiar humming and the crunch of gravel.

"Daddy's home!" I said excitedly, standing up and running to the front door with Mary Ellen close behind.

"Daddy's home! Daddy's home!" screamed the Monster, wriggling her head under my arm as I cracked the door open and, through the diced world of the screen door, watched the pickup truck roll to a stop alongside the house. The headlights were still on, glaring harshly. Inside the cab I could only make out a featureless, looming mass of shadow, a dense block of dark fixed between the deep purple of the early evening sky and the white shafts of the headlights. A second later the light snapped off and there was stillness. Slowly, the truck door opened and boomed shut and a huge form, still blackened in shadow and towering up into the sky, strode towards us. With three giant strides it was hanging above our heads and suddenly my dad's red massive face shone wild in the pale light thrown off by the front door lamp, his beard as big and thick as a hedge, blue eyes glinting steely and untamed and hard out of the night.

"Daddy!" I called to him.

"Hi, daddy-daddy-daddy-o!" yelled Mary Ellen, jumping up and down.

"Out of the way for Christ sakes!" roared my dad, "you're blockin' the god dammed door. Can't a man get into his own damn house? Jesus!" and one of his giant boots rose up into the air, higher than Mary Ellen's head, I thought, and crashed down into the doorway as his bulky frame pushed past us and shouldered in through the front door, miraculously without ripping away the frame.

The room shrank as my dad entered, hurling his coat and steel lunch pail onto a chair and dropping hugely down at the head of the table.

"Jesus H. Christ," he growled, "what a day. I'm hungry as hell."

My mother was already up, filling a plate full of food. Mary Ellen and I crept into a corner of the kitchen, awed and stunned into silence. Again. Quietly, we watched my mom placing the laden plate in front of my dad, then go over to the cabinet filled with bottles and glasses.

"What the hell's this?" demanded my dad.

"It's got bacon in it," said my mom, her back to him. "You want a twist of lemon in your gin?"

"Yeah," said my dad, sniffing at his food before shoveling a huge portion into his mouth. I watched his giant jaw muscles working as he chewed, a solid knot of rock rippling under the red skin, blue eyes catching the light like thin sheets of metal, flashing. The gin gulped into the glass, tonic water fizzled happily and a cube of ice cracked loudly as it plopped in.

My mom brought the glass over and set it into one of my dad's thick, scarred hands, crowned with black and broken fingernails. He drank, said, "Christ," and drank again.

"Hard day, huh?" My mom's voice was a cooing, lulling half-whispered song.

"Christ yeah. A real bastard. Goddamned cable busted on the rig and me and Mike spent all god damned mornin' tryin' to fit on another." He stuffed more food into his mouth. "What is this?"

"It's made with cheese. The kids have noticed that Taffy's pregnant," continued the smooth, even, melodic voice coming out of my mom. "When do you think she'll have them?"

My dad drank some more, and you could see his body starting to unfreeze, the shoulders losing some of their tension, the jaw muscles unknotting themselves and the fierce cold flaming eyes warming and mellowing slightly. Now his lined faced seemed to sag, and all his 55 hard years in this world showed clearly on his wrinkled face, his graying hair, his scruffy beard.

"Any day now, I figure. Then we'll have a whole damn family of dogs, huh Mary Ellen?" This was the first time he had noticed we were in the room. "What is this stuff anyways, honey?"

"Cheese and bacon pie." Twenty years younger than my dad, she looked more like his daughter than his wife.

"It ain't bad. You make it before?"

"No, it's a new recipe."

"What's that?" My dad turned his bad ear away from my mom.

"New recipe," she said loudly.

"Oh. Ain't half bad but you know what I'd really like sometimes? Grits. Some of them grits and ham and hominy. That's a goddamned good meal for you, boy. Hell, my mother used to cook that all the time, and the whole neighborhood used to wish they was in our family to get some. You should make that sometimes, honey."

My mom was up and piling more salad onto my dad's plate. He reached behind him to the gin bottle and the tonic water and made himself another drink.

"What are we going to do with the puppies?"

"Let's keep 'em," I said, approaching the table and sitting down next to my dad. Waves of heat rose up off his skin and a certain smell, a mixture of pipe smoke, sweat, grease and dirt and blood, blocked out the kitchen smells and filled my nostrils.

"Guess we'll just hafta drown 'em." My dad winked at me.

"Oh no!" whimpered Mary Ellen, running to my dad and throwing her arms around him. "They're babies, daddy. They're only babies."

"Your father's only joking," said my mom, "he wouldn't do anything bad to them."

My dad picked Mary Ellen up. "Oh Christ," he said, "you're gettin' to be a big girl, ain'tcha?" He pushed his plate towards the center of the table. "Fill'er up with more, honey. That tastes pretty damn good."

My mom stood up, with a tiny golden light dancing in the deep dark brown pools of her eyes. The barest flicker of a smile played around the corners of her mouth as she turned her face away from my dad.

"It's called quiche," she said, loading more food onto my dad's plate. "And it comes from France."

3

I was awakened in the morning by the silken rays of a smiling sun on my face, which had very gently drawn me out of sleep. I stayed in bed for quite a while, staring up at the sky and the hills, watching the sunshine with the happy knowledge that school was months and months, years away and that the blue of the sky was unending, as were the summer days. I was half convinced that the night had never even come and it was always daytime in the summer and that the only way changes of time could be registered was by the movement of the hands on people's watches and by the different shades of blue in the sky.

These thoughts vanished with the sound of my mom's voice. "Del," she was saying, "get up. Telephone for you."

Lazily, I got out of bed and walked out into the hallway where the telephone receiver lay off the hook on a small table. "Hello?"

"Hi buttface. Still asleep?"

"Shuddup, jerk."

"You just get up?" It was Davy.

"Yup. It's summer, you know."

"Geez. Halfta day's gone. Whatcha up to today?"

"Nuthin'. You?"

"Nuthin'."

"Why don'tcha come on over here then," I suggested through a yawn. "You've never ever been here before. We can work on our models or somethin'."

"OK, that sounds neato. Jeet jet?"

"Yeah, I had some toast in bed," I lied.

"Alright, I'll be over in a half hour or somethin'. I gotta ask my mom first."

"OK, see ya soon--and don't forget to bring a kit."

"I know," said Davy, and then in a whisper he said, "I got somethin' to show ya, too."

"What?" I asked, waking up.

"You'll see. Bye." There was a dead buzzing in my ear.

Placing the receiver back on the hook, I ran full blast into my room where I jumped into jeans and a t-shirt, then ran into the kitchen to gulp down a bowl of granola. While I was eating, my mom came walking through, carrying a laundry basket piled high with dirty clothes.

"Hi," I said, mouth dripping with milk. "That was Davy on the phone. It is OK if he comes over today?"

"A bit late to ask, isn't it? I'm sure he's on his way now."

"That's not fair," I smiled, "you always figure out everythin'."

"Special radar. Davy can have lunch with us too, if he likes."

"I'll ask 'im."

At that moment, Kathy walked in. Her hair was a tangled mass and her eyes were puffy and red. She was wearing only a pajama top which barely reached the tops of her thighs. I hated to see my sister exposed that way and I looked away. It was embarrassing. But I managed to say, "Hi."

"Where's the milk?"

"It's right here, sleepy, I got it."

My mom left the kitchen with the basket, but returned a second later, empty-handed. One look at her and I knew something was going to happen. Her mouth was a thin, pale line drawn straight across her face and it looked as though all the blood had been drained from her head. Her dark brown eyes had turned into shiny black marbles, hard and cold.

"I want to talk with you, Kathleen," she said without parting her lips.

Kathy turned around and folded her arms across her chest, leaning against the counter. Her face was set and pinched.

"I thought I told you to be in at nine o'clock last night," hissed my mom.

Kathy stared at her.

"As long as you're under this roof, young lady, and eating my food, you will obey me. Do I make myself clear?"

"The car broke down."

"Where?"

"In Atascadero."

"Why didn't you call?"

"I didn't have a dime."

"And the other girls?"

"What others?" said Kathy with a sarcastic tone in her voice. An instant later, her face began to redden.

My mom took a step towards her, head down. "You told me you were with Peggy and Shelly." My mom's eyes scoped down into two fine steel drills and started spinning.

"We--I was. I mean, we were all together. With Ernie." Kathy was trying to make her voice sound sullen and bored, but her scarlet face was giving her away. "And then they--Peggy and Shelly--they took off."

"How did they get home without a car?"

"They--I don't know how, OK?" Kathy's voice rose.

My mom took another step towards her, finger jabbing at her chest. "You listen to me, Kathleen. Do not raise your voice to me or you'll regret it, is that clear?" Kathy's head nodded just slightly. Her body suddenly looked shrunken to me. "Now, if you want to go out," my mom continued, "with some boy or whomever, then I expect you to come home when I say, understand? When you're grown and on your own, fine. Then you can get a job and an apartment and do whatever you like with whomever you like. But when your feet are under this table, you play by the rules. It's that simple. I'm the one who has to deal with your father's temper, not you, and I will not allow you to make my job any more difficult than it already is, understand?" Kathy stared at my mom, then nodded sullenly. My mom glared back at her with fiery, unblinking eyes and I could see one of her fingers trembling slightly; for a second I thought she was going to hit Kathy, but then her shoulders dropped and she turned and went out of the room.

Kathy stood still for a while, staring into the space where my mom had been, then put her hand on her forehead and said, "Shit."

"Taffy's gonna have puppies," I offered, but Kathy did not answer. She didn't even look at me. She walked quickly away, slamming the kitchen door behind her.

I continued to eat, peacefully. This show was nothing new to me. Kathy was always arguing with my parents. She always lost, too. Half the time she deserved to lose because she was so single-minded and block-headed. Just like General Custer, she'd never succeed with a blunt, head-on assault. She never seemed to understand that it's dangerous to grow up around your parents. Sometimes they're really dumb, but other times they can be clever and tricky and downright sneaky. So you got to outsmart them, keep one step ahead, or you'll get caught and that means getting punished. That was a thing to be avoided at all costs. Kathy never understood this. She only learned through one way: the hardest.

Raising my bowl, I drank the last of the milk and nuts and toasted oats and, lowering it onto the table again, I saw a dark blue station wagon snaking up the dirt road to our place and throwing up a long trail of yellow dust behind it. I lost sight of it when it rounded the bend to climb up the little incline to our house. I placed my spoon and the bowl into the sink and went to the screen door from where I watched the car crunch to a stop and the passenger door open almost immediately. Out stepped Davy, a medium-sized, well-built boy with straight sandy brown hair, blue eyes and a pug nose. He was wearing worn jeans, sneakers and a t-shirt with broad horizontal stripes running across it. A small green army surplus bag was held tightly under one arm as if he was afraid somebody would try and take it from him. My mom followed me out to the car.

"Hello, Mrs. Turner."

"Morning Mrs. Peterson," my mom replied.

"David, greet your hostess."

"Hi, Mrs. Turner," he said, smiling.

"Good morning," corrected Davy's mom.

"Good morning," repeated Davy, eyes rolling upwards. He came up to me, grinning and leaned over close. "Wait'll ya see what I got with me," he whispered.

"You're getting to be a big boy now aren't you?" my mom asked.

Davy shrugged. "Guess so."

Mrs. Peterson's eyes glinted in the harsh morning sun like steel darts. "I know you can speak better than that, young man," she said, her face squished up like she had just taken a bite of lemon. Her eyes, nose and mouth soured into a tight ball of displeasure.

Davy sighed. "I'm exactly three-quarters of an inch taller."

"You could stand up a bit straighter as well, so you don't ruin your posture." Mrs. Peterson looked at my mom, shaking her head. "These boys," she said.

My mom only laughed weakly for an answer, then ran her hand through my hair, and with the other patted Davy on the head. "Well," was all she said.

Mrs. Peterson glanced at her watch. "I really must get going. David, you behave yourself. I don't want to hear anything bad about you, do I make myself clear?"

Davy rolled his eyes. "Yup."

"What did you say?"

"Yes, mother."

"That's better. Mrs. Turner, I'll pick him up at five-thirty sharp, if that's alright with you."

"That'll be fine."

"Good. I wish you a lovely day, then," said Mrs. Peterson to my mother. She nodded silently at me, then glared at Davy for a long second. Finally, the engine started up and she was gone. Every time she left our place I had an enormous desire to let out a long, "*Whew.*"

My mom turned and looked at us. "So, boys, what are you up to today?"

"Oh, just messin' around and stuff."

"Yeah, I brought a model with me and we're gonna work on it together, huh Del, in your room."

"Oh, come now. You don't want to be cooped up inside on such a fine day do you?"

29

"I really wanna get started on this model, Mrs. Turner," said Davy, "It's a new *Panzer Mark IV* and it's really neat." Davy tugged on my sleeve. "C'mon," he said with a touch of urgency in his voice, "let's go and get started, huh?"

"OK," and we both ran off to my room. Once inside, Davy sat down on the floor, hugging his army bag close to his body. "Shut that door, will ya?" he said, "And come over here and look."

I closed the door and sat down next to Davy, Indian-style. "Boy are you actin' all secretive this mornin'," I said.

"Shuddup. Look at what I got," said Davy, reaching slowly into his bag. He brought out two thick magazines. I could only see the cigarette ads on the backs of them because Davy held them against his chest, his mouth slightly open and his eyes wide. He seemed to be listening for something.

"What's that mags?"

"*Shhhh*. Is someone coming?"

I cocked my head sideways, listening. "No, you nut. What's the prob? Why are your so nervous?"

"Lock the door, will ya?"

"Why? You're weird."

"Just lock it OK, or I won't show you what I got."

Making a *tch* sound with my tongue, I stood up, secured the door and sat down again. "OK," I said, "stop screwin' around now. What's the big secret?"

A small, devious smile was just visible on Davy's lips as he slowly lowered the magazines and spread them on the floor. "Look," he said.

My mouth fell open and a small fury animal leaped inside my stomach. "Holy kamoly, Davy," I whispered hoarsely, "where'd you get these?" I was not looking at Davy as I spoke. My eyes were fixed on the two cover women smiling up at me. Their eyes were dark and almond-shaped and dreamily fluid. Their long, brunette hair fell softly over exposed shoulders and barely covered the heavy swell of their smooth, full breasts. One was sitting on the hood of a red sports car with her legs crossed, the other was on a balcony, leaning over a carved wooden railing and looking right at me, one bare breast aimed directly at my mouth, which was watering. Come, her eyes purred, come to me.

"I copped 'em from my dad," Davy was saying to me, his voice muffled and faint, like he was speaking under a blanket. My head spun in slow revolutions. "He's got a whole stack of 'em hid up in our attic. But I found 'em."

"Uh-huh," I mumbled, thumbing through the one with the woman leaning over the fence.

Silently, blissfully, intensely, I went through the magazine. It was some sort of special issue because it had a gallery of women who each represented a month. I stopped at Miss April, in love. Holding the page up close to my face, I whistled between my teeth. "Wow," I said. After several minutes, I lowered the magazine and looked into Davy's face. "What if your dad and mom find out?"

"They won't," said Davy, his eyes buried into the other magazine. "But just in case, is it alright if I leave 'em here for a while? You know, just in case."

My heart leapt and my tongue involuntarily flicked out over dry lips. "Sure." I tried to make my voice sound casual and disinterested.

"I mean, just in case. You know what a loony my mom can be sometimes. If she caught me with these I'd be grounded for the next twenty years."

"No prob," I said, more recovered now. "I can stash 'em here. Nobody'd find 'em. Even my mom doesn't come in here without askin'."

"Great. I wish my mom was like that."

"Wow," I said almost to myself, feeling a gently glowing pool of warmth spreading inside me as I looked at the magazine again. "This is great."

There was a noise outside the door and my heart abruptly shut off. For one terrible second my entire body was rigid with fear, but a moment later it exploded with urgent, screaming frantic energy. I sprang up, grabbed both magazines, rushed over to the dresser and crammed them inside. Then I spun around, staring with wide eyes at the door. Davy sat still on the floor, his face a shade whiter than normal. We watched the door for several seconds, breathing in thin wisps.

After a while Davy said, "Nothin'."

"Yeah. Guess it was just a noise or somethin'. Boy, I almost had a heart attack." I walked over to the door, unlocked it and went back to Davy. "What other goodies you got in your bag?"

"The *Mark IV*."

"You mean you actually brought a model along?"

"Yup. No lie. C'mon, let's work on 'em for a while."

"Alright. I think we oughta leave the mags where they are, huh? We can look at 'em some other time. Look what I got the other day."

I went over to my desk at the window, picked up a box and showed the cover to Davy.

"Get outta here," he said, "I hate that old stuff. World War II's much neater."

"No way. You got no kind of appreciation. These old airplanes from the First World War are the bestest. And you gotta have more skill to build 'em." I sat down next to Davy, who had opened his box and was fingering the smooth polystyrene parts, molded crisply and cleanly and delicately on the plastic trees on which they had been formed. Silently, we bent our heads, armed ourselves with modeling knives, and went to work.

Outside my window, the morning was unfolding majestically. Sunlight dripped down from its unseen source, honeying the windowsill, catching the shape of the window frame and casting golden boxes of light onto the wooden floor of my room. The air inside was warm and it smelled good, a summer smell of flowers and dried grass. Occasionally, I glanced up at Davy, his shoulders hunched, his head bent, a lock of sandy hair hanging down over his eyes, his small, white teeth sinking into his lower lip as he worked on his model with concentration. His skin was unblemished and velvety, plumpened by the very last vestiges of baby fat which would soon be burned off by the consuming energies of this life. But now the skin still retained a certain purity; there were no lines of worry or grief, no scars, no tautness, only a shine, a candle glow emanating from the fine boyish face.

My attention refocused on the kit. Carefully I cut the wings, struts and fuselage halves from their plastic spurs and with sandpaper smoothed down their edges. I dry-fit the model, snapping pieces together without glue to get an idea of how it all went together. Pulling another shoebox out from under my desk, I fingered through little tins of black, white, and olive drab, selecting those colors which I would use to paint the bi-plane.

"Hey," said Davy, causing me to look up. He lay flat on his back on the floor, with his hands on his stomach, fingers tapping silently. "I'm sick of buildin' models," he told the ceiling.

Yawning, I curved my back, bent my arms and stretched. "Yeah, I guess me, too." I put my modeling knife into the shoebox with the paints, and lay on my side, my head resting inside the palm of my hand.

"So whaddya wanna do now?" said Davy.

"I dunna know. Whaddya wanna do?"

"I dunno."

"Me neither. Wanna play soldiers?" I asked.

"Naw."

"We could ride bikes."

"Don't wanna."

"I got darts."

"Uh-uh."

"Well, what do you wanna do?"

"I dunno. I know what."

"What?"

"How 'bout Secret Service, down at the barn?"

I sat up, sleep draining out of my head. "Alright."

"Who for?"

"Whodaya think?"

"Bobby?"

"Yup."

"Great," said Davy, getting up. "You got guns?"

"Right behind you, dummy." Davy twisted around and grabbed the two plastic squirt guns while I rummaged through a large wooden box filled with comics and old t-shirts, tennis balls and stuffed animals, and found a tin sheriff's badge I had won at the county fair last summer. I pinned it over my left breast.

"You can't wear the badge there, numbnuts," said Davy. "We're

Secret Service. You gotta stick it in your pocket, then flash it when you need to. But it's gotta be all secret-like."

"Yeah, OK. Gimmie a gun. No, I want the blue one." I slipped the water pistol and the badge into my back pocket. "Good. Let's go."

We went outside, stopping by a faucet to fill up our guns. As I replaced the rubber plug back into my pistol, I caught a glimpse of the Monster crawling on all fours into the pole barn. "Hey," I turned to Davy, "there goes my little sister. Let's follow her and arrest her."

"Yeah."

Stepping gingerly across the rocky driveway, we stole up to the barn, dark and cool inside and smelling strongly of diesel oil, grease and sawdust. Motioning to Davy, I pulled my pistol out and crept inside, eyes wide and watchful. Then I raised a hand and we both stopped. "Look," I whispered, pointing at the Monster. She was squatting on her haunches now, and watching something underneath one of my dad's trucks. Signaling with my hand, Davy and I raised our guns and moved forward. I waited until we were directly behind the Monster.

"Secret Service," I said, "You're under arrest."

"Shuddup," said the Monster, not bothering to look around.

"Freeze or we shoot."

"*Shhhhhh* you guys. She's actin' weird."

"Who's actin' weird?" I asked Mary Ellen, kneeling down beside her.

She pointed. "Just lookit."

I had to drop on my hands and knees to get down low enough to see under the truck. It was murky and dark and I saw nothing at first but then there were two shiny points of light sparkling at me out of the black. I blinked and my eyes, now adjusted to the light, picked out the long, conical face of Taffy, slopping down into the sharp black nose. She didn't bark or whine or growl or anything. She only stared at me.

"What's she doin'?" asked Davy, now along side me.

"Nuthin'. She's just sitting there in the dark. It's weird alright."

"Maybe it's cause she's pregnant that's why she's actin' all weird and she's like tryin' to find a place dark and quiet to have the puppies."

"But she'll get cold under there," said the Monster.

"No she won't," scoffed Davy, "she's gotta fur coat on."

"Maybe we should make her a bed or somethin'."

I considered this for a moment. "Yeah, Mary Ellen. That's not a half bad idea. We could get some old rags and stuff and make a nice cozy place for her to have the puppies in. Sure beat lyin' under dad's truck in the dark like this."

"Yeah, let's go ask mom," said Mary Ellen and we trooped off to the house where we found my mom ensconced on the couch, reading a book about Lord Byron. We told her our idea and she told us we could use some old towels which she kept under the sink in the kitchen. Having gotten these, we returned to the pole barn. Davy stuck his head under the truck. "Yup," he informed us, "she's still under there alright." Taking an old wooden crate, we turned it over onto one side, butted it up against an inside wall of the barn--out of the way of my dad's trucks--and laid out the towels to make a bed.

The Monster squatted down and looked under the truck. "Come, Taffy," she called, "come girl, come."

"Aw, leave her alone," I said, "She'll come out when she's good and ready."

"Yeah. She'll find the bed by herself."

But the Monster stubbornly ignored us and she continued to plead at the dog.

I jerked my head at Davy, saying, "C'mon, let's go to the horse barn."

To get to the other barn, you had to crawl under the wooden fence which encircled our house and the driveway, climb down a steep but short slope and walk across a broad pasture. The pasture was grassy and very flat. You had to be careful when you crossed it because of the many gopher holes which pocked its surface, and also wasp's nests. One time Kathy had stumbled on one of these underground nests and a black roaring cloud of angry insects swarmed up out of the earth and stung her all over her back and arms.

"Watch out for the wasps," I told Davy, trying to make my voice sound deep and grave. He was from the town down on the coast and I enjoyed using my knowledge of the country to scare him. "If you step on a wasp hole, they'll fly up out of the ground and sting your eyes out of your head and you'll be blinded."

"Nah-uh. You're just trying to fake me out," said Davy, eyeing the ground carefully.

I rilled my tongue against the roof of my mouth. "And if you hear that sound, freeze. Don't move a muscle."

"Why come?"

"'Cause that means you've stepped on a rattlesnake and its gettin' ready to bite you and if you move one inch it'll strike and you'll be so scared your heart'll pump the poison into your brain and you'll turn purple and start barfin' and then you'll die."

"Get outta here. You're makin' all this stuff up." Davy paused. "Aren'tcha?"

"Just walk real careful, like me," I said, placing my feet with precision as I slowly crept ahead. I smiled to myself as Davy, eyes wide and mouth open, followed my every move.

Suddenly he screamed and flew up into the air as my body jumped in terror. Then he began madly hopping around on one leg with the other extended out in front of him, shaking wildly. "Ahhh!" Davy screamed, "a snake, a snake, it's crawling up my leg!"

Horrified, I ran up to him and began beating his upper thigh, trying to kill the rattler before it could strike. "Keep still you idiot!" I yelled at him, my heart pounding and my voice breaking with fear. "We gotta kill it," and I drummed on his leg with both fists.

Davy stopped hopping and, balancing on one leg, shook the other one vigorously. Something slid out of his pants' leg and dropped onto the brown earth.

"Look out!" I shouted, its right there!" and Davy sprang backwards. Cautiously, I bent down, peering closely at the snake. A second later I stood up straight. "You city slickerin' dummy," I said with disgust. "That wasn't no rattler, it was only a little old lizard."

Davy rubbed his hand up and down his leg. "Well it sure felt like a rattler. It was all creepy feelin' and stuff."

"Poor little guy," I said, stooping again. "He's dead."

"That'll teach 'em to scare people."

"Shuddup. C'mon, let's give 'im a burial at least."

Davy was still rubbing his leg. "It was all scaly and had little sharp things and it felt really creepy goin' up my leg like that," he kept saying as we dug a tiny hole in the soft earth, placed the lizard inside and covered it up again. "Geez, what a creepy feelin'," said Davy as I broke a twig to make a cross and stuck it into the fresh mound. I placed a large stone on the grave. "There," I said wiping the dirt off my hands, "we can find it later on in a couple of months and dig 'im up and have a lizard skeleton."

"Neato," said Davy.

We ran the rest of the way to the railroad tie-and-pine fence surrounding the horse barn, scrambled over it and walked across the center of the corral to the barn. Smokey, a large appaloosa with hooves the size of a Clydesdale and a fierce temperament, snorted at us defiantly and turned his head sideways to watch us as we made for the haystack.

"Hey, he's lookin' at us," said Davy, moving up close to me.

"Aw, it's alright. Smokey won't hurt you. He's a friendly guy."

Smokey snorted again, lowered his great head and slowly headed toward us, tail swishing the flies away from him. Putting out my hand, I rubbed his snout as he came up to us, and scratched his forehead and big, solid neck. "Go on Davy, give 'im a pat. He won't hurt you."

"Wow," said Davy, tentatively petting the horse. "I've never been so close to a real live horse before. He's hugeacious."

"18 hands high."

"What's that mean?"

"That's cowboy talk. It means he's really big."

After that we opened a wooden door and entered the hay stall. The bales, golden yellow and sweetly scented, were piled high to the ceiling. You could smell the leather saddles and harnesses from the tack room next door, and Smokey's sweet horse smell, and the fine dust rising up off the hay and the powdered earthen floor which mingled with the scent of the redwood barn.

"Secret Agents!" cried out Davy and together we hunted the Bad Guys who wanted to do bad things to Bobby Kennedy. The Bad Guys hung around in the dark spaces between the bales of hay, or up in the rafters where we found a bird's nest and Davy squirted one in the tack room as he crouched behind a saddle, and I wounded his partner, but the other two got away out through the window. Those Bad Guys could really be slippery sometimes. After about an hour, Davy said, "I'm tired of this. Let's play war now."

"OK. Which one?"

"Vietnam."

"Ah, c'mon, we always play that. Why not World War I?"

"No," protested Davy. "I wanna play Vietnam. It's our war and my big brother's over there in the Marines and he's a real live hero and stuff and besides we played your stupid Bobby game so now we can play mine."

"OK," and we sneaked out of the tack room on our bellies, eyes watchful for Vietcong. We fought them around the corner of the barn and had a pitched battle in the Mekong Delta--Smokey's water trough--and Davy got a flesh wound in the shoulder but he didn't die.

The day lengthened and the game petered out. I was dirty, tired and hungry. We stopped at the hose near Smokey's water and drank, the cool, icy freshness cutting through the layer of dust lining our throats. Then we walked back slowly through the pasture. The summer sun was still high in the vault of blueness, but had softened, turning the grass' fading green into deep emerald, and the earth into a toasty golden brown. The heavy air was warm and fragrant and there was no breeze. Everything was still, except for the occasional butterfly which flittered past faint and shimmering in the glowing light. Davy kept turning his head, scanning and rescanning every bit of ground before he would place his foot down.

"Know what?"

"What?" asked Davy, not lifting his eyes from the ground.

"You oughta spend the night tonight."

Davy walked on a couple more careful steps. "I don't think my parents'd let me. My mom, I mean."

"Why not? Just ask her. You can call 'em when we get back."

"Naw. She'll say no. She always says no. That's how she is."

"I know what let's do. We'll get my mom to ask."

Davy took his eyes off the ground for a second to look at me. "Yeah?"

"Sure. If she calls, then it'll sound more official like and your parents--I mean your mom--won't be able to say no and you can stay over."

"Gee, that'd be great. I just hope my mom--"

"Forget about her. Then tomorrow we can pack a lunch and stuff and go explorin' and maybe visit Ritchie Lane over the hill."

"Who's that?"

"This rock star guy who lives over there," I made a vague sweeping gesture with my arm, "and he's gotta neat place with a real-life tepee and stuff. He's a Hippy."

"Wow. A real-life Hippy. My mom'll kill me."

"Neato!"

"Neato!"

We reached the house, me leading Davy into the kitchen where my mom sat at the table, reading as usual.

"Hi, mom."

She put the book down and took off her glasses. "Hello there boys. Don't you two look a mess. What have you been doing, rolling in the dirt?"

"Yup," I said cheerfully. "We were at the horse barn."

"'Yes,'" my mom corrected. "Well, go wash up and then come and eat. I've already cooked so you can have dinner now. You'll be eating too, won't you Davy?"

"Yes, Mrs. Turner."

I looked at Davy. "You go wash first. You know where the bathroom is." When he was gone, I turned towards my mom. "Mom, could you do me a most excellent favor?"

My mom looked at me out of the corner of her eyes. "Tell me what it is first."

"Could you maybe call up Davy's mom and ask her if like it's alright if Davy spends the night tonight? We figured like maybe it'd be better for you to call 'cause if Davy does she'll say no for sure. Please."

"OK, Del. And then perhaps you and Davy could pull a few weeds in the garden tomorrow, huh?"

"Aw, mom. It's summer--"

"It's a *quid pro quo*."

"It's a squid-crow who?"

"*Quid pro quo*. That's Latin for I scratch your back, you scratch mine."

I considered this for a moment. "Yeah, well, alright, I guess. I guess we can work in the garden for a while. So will you call?"

"I'll phone her right now. You go wash up."

"Great!" I said, running down the hall to the bathroom.

When I returned, Davy was already seated at the table. He beamed at me as I sat down opposite him.

"Guess what!"

"What?"

"Your mom says my mom says I can stay over for two whole days."

"Wow wee!"

"Yeah, we can do all kinda stuff now!"

"Yup. Tomorrow let's get up early and go hikin' in the hills. We can take a backpack with lunch and stuff and my BB gun."

"Great!"

My mom approached the table and laid two steaming bowls in front of Davy and me, filled with chunks of meat and halved potatoes, sliced carrots and onions all swimming in a thick reddish brown sauce that smelled strongly of wine, basil and garlic. Davy stared into the bowl for a second, nostrils twitching. Then he picked up his spoon and stuck it into his bowl.

"Go ahead, Davy," I said with a full mouth. "It ain't poison."

"'Isn't'," came from my mom.

"Isn't. Whaddaya call this this time?" I asked her.

"*Boeuf Bourguignon*, another French dish."

"Jeepers!" said Davy. "This tastes great. Is it from a store or somethin'?"

My mom, her eyes like lasers, opened her mouth to speak but I was quicker. "No way. It's fresh cooked."

"Wow. You guys always eat like this?"

"Uh-huh."

"Jeepers! I usually only get hot dogs and pork n' beans from a can. You sure this ain't frozen?"

"Certainly not," snapped my mom.

"Jeepers!" said Davy, eating like a starved boy.

40

We finished our meal, then went into the living room where, with full bellies and droopy eyes, we flicked through the TV, staring open-mouthed at talking cigarettes, a bald man with muscles and an earring, pristine housewives scrubbing gleaming linoleum floors, and talking dogs. One channel had the news on and we awakened suddenly to watch a report by a journalist in a tan short-sleeved shirt with straps on the shoulders talking about the war, while behind him we saw giant olive green trucks and low-bellied tanks and in the distance a helicopter. Davy looked for his brother, but we couldn't find him. After that Bobby Kennedy was on because of some primary somewhere, and then there were reports about Eugene McCarthy, Humphrey and Nixon, too, but they didn't interest me much. When the RFK report was on, I got up and stood in the hall and shouted, "Mom! Bobby Kennedy's on TV!" An instant later, I heard the light, rapid footsteps of my mother. She rushed in, wiping her hands on a towel and stood near the couch, leaning forward slightly, her eyes bright and sharp. When the report was over, she shook her head and sighed, "What a man," and left.

"She's a fan," I explained to Davy.

"Not my mom. She don't like 'im. She's says he's a nigger lover."

"Hey shuddup. My mom doesn't allow that word in our house. At least when my dad's not around."

"But he is," insisted Davy. "She says all the Kennedy's are screwed up that way."

"Then why do you play Secret Service for Bobby then?"

"'Cause."

"'Cause what?"

"'Cause you wouldn't never play it about anybody else and if I said Nixon or Humphrey you'd say no and we'd start fightin' and never play anythin'. That's 'cause."

"Well," I said. "You're just not supposed to use that word--"

"What word?"

"--shuddup--in our house and if my mom hears ya, you're gonna get yelled at and she'll send you home."

"Somebody's here'," said Davy, standing up and going over to a window which looked out on the driveway. I followed.

"That's my dad. He must've just drove up."

"That's your dad? Jeepers. He's kinda scary lookin'."

"He's just tired from work is all. He's not so scary when he gets to relax."

"Aren't you gonna go say hi?"

"Naw. He'll just scream at me. My mom says he needs his fifteen minutes of peace to forget all about what a hard day he had." I didn't mention the gin tonics.

We stayed in the living room, flicking through TV channels, making dull, lethargic TV-drained comments to each other. After about an hour or so, we heard someone walking heavily down the hallway. A rapid, powerful solid step. I slid out of the big chair, and onto the floor. Davy was watching the black mouth of the hall like he was expecting Frankenstein's monster to come marching out of it. The footsteps grew louder and my dad strode into the room and headed straight to the big chair which he slumped leadenly into, a shot glass full of *Canadian Club* in one of his blistered paws.

"What the hell's that you're watchin'?"

"*Get Smart*," I said, "It's almost over."

"*Get Smart*? Hell, you don't wanna watch that."

"It's almost over."

"I hate that skinny bastard, don't you? He ain't funny. Where's the remote control?"

Davy swallowed hard. "Here sir. I have it," he whispered, handing it to my dad, who was closely peering at Davy.

"Who the hell are you?"

Davy took a step back as my dad pressed the remote control and found a show he wanted to watch.

"That's Davy," I answered for my friend. "We go to school together."

"Sit down, boy and shut your mouth. You tryin' to catch a fly or somethin'?" smiled my dad. Davy shut his mouth, not realizing that my dad was joking with him. "What's your dad do, Gary?"

"Davy," I said.

"Um, he's an engineer at P,G & E."

"What's that?" said my dad, leaning his good ear towards Davy.

"Engineer at P,G & E in Morro Bay, sir."

"Why the hell you keep sayin' 'sir'? This ain't the army. What's yer last name?" My dad took a sip of whiskey.

"P-P-Peterson."

"Huh?"

"Peterson," I answered for Davy in a loud voice. Davy sat down on the sofa with his knees pressed together and his hands in his lap.

"Peterson? Oh, hell yes. You're old man's an engineer at the gas and electric company." My dad said this to the TV. He was watching a special report about riots in Detroit. "Looka those crazy sonofabitches. The whole country's gettin' took over by long hairs and niggers. Its drugs is what's doin' it. It wasn't this way when I was a boy. Shit."

"Look at those cops wailin' on people." I said.

"What?"

I sucked in a deep breath and raised my voice. "I said, those cops are really beatin' on people."

My dad laughed grimly and drank from his glass. "They're sonofabitches, too. Cops are the biggest bunch of crooks there is. Can't trust 'em. Always on the take. Ain't like when I was a kid, boy. Back in Dayton, we used to leave our goddamned doors unlocked, the whole damn neighborhood. Weren't no drugs, no Hippies and that loud music..." I silently rose to my feet as my dad lectured the TV. I caught Davy's eye and he stood up, too. "...cops were sonofabitches too, but you could trust the bastards more than nowadays and my mother used to sit out on the porch 'cause we had a radio in our house, the first house in the whole damn neighborhood and everybody would come up to our place to listen to it 'cause ain't nobody else had one but us and there was a time when old Harry O'Toole, a fat sonofabitch from Boston come up..."

Davy and I were out of the living room and running down the hall. We cut through the kitchen where my mom sat reading. Jogging past her she said—without lifting her head or taking her eyes off the page—"You boys get ready for bed. And don't run in the house."

As we walked the rest of the way to my bedroom, Davy turned to me. "That's about the most swear words I ever heard in my life."

"That's just how my dad talks. He doesn't mean anythin' by it."

"I think he's even scarier up close."

"Naw," I said. "He's alright. He likes you. Just don't get him mad at you, like my dumb older sister does. That's the trick."

"Why'd we run out of the room like that?"

"'Cause *Get Smart* was over. And also I hate it when my dad starts talkin' about the old days. It's borin' and he won't stop and he always tells the same stories again and again 'til you wanna scream." We were in my bedroom now, and I was sitting on the edge of the bed, pulling my boots off. My mom had been in earlier and had set up a cot for Davy. He sat down on it, yawned and rubbed his stomach. "Wanna hit the sack?" I asked him.

"May's well. I'm beat."

"Me too. Besides, we gotta lot to do tomorrow. You think maybe I should set the alarm so we can get an early start?"

"No. Well, OK. I guess we oughta. I just hate alarms 'cause they remind me of school."

"Yeah, I know. But we should do it so we don't sleep too late."

Davy's mouth was stretched wide in a huge yawn. "OK," he managed to say without closing it.

I stripped off all my clothing, switched off the light and hopped into bed, coiling up into a tight ball as the chilly tongues of the bed sheets licked my skin. There was a full moon out and I punched my pillow and sat up against it, looking out into the silvery blackness. The dark gray outline of the hills to the east shimmered, and the tree branches outside my window twisted themselves into writhing black worms reaching out into the night, their thin bodies disappearing into darkness.

"Davy?" I said to the moon. "You asleep?"

"Almost." His voice was faint.

"You gonna get in trouble 'cause you're spendin' the night?"

"Probably. I always get in trouble."

"That's rotten. They're not gonna wup you, are they?"

"Might," said Davy weakly. "Might not. Depends on their moods. My mom's mood, I mean."

"That's not right. They--your mom--should just let you be. We just wanna have fun."

There was no answer.

"Davy?" My voice sounded loud in the silence. "Night," I whispered. Rolling onto my side, I drew my knees up to my chest and tucked my chin down. Against the lids of my closed eyes I could see the flickering dance and play of moonlight. Upon this gossamer screen was projected the women of the magazine that Davy had brought with him this morning. Beautiful April and August, December darkly, sweet June. The large brown eyes, breasts large and heavy, long silken hair, smooth thighs. My body warmed, my breath deepened, palms slick with sweat, hand descending, moonlight like silver painted on my eyeballs, hot breath now in surrounding warmth, quickening breath, breathing through my mouth, and then a shuddering and everything was white light silver changing gray into black.

4

I woke up very early the next morning and reached over to switch off the alarm clock. On my back in the warm bed, toes wiggling, hands clasped across my chest, I closed my eyes and tried to remember a dream I had had in the night. Voices, a winged something flapping across darkness, elongated grinning faces: only the fragments were left, nothing else would come up to me from what had happened in my sleep. I tried to fall back again, to return and capture the essences of these images, but the small of my back started hurting and when I rolled over onto my side, it throbbed dully with a deep ache and sleep would not come. Then I felt tremendously thirsty, so I flung off the blankets and pulled on my jeans. Creeping over to Davy's cot I saw that he was peacefully far away in sleepness, so I picked one of my socks off the floor and laid it carefully on his forehead. Then I slipped out the door and walked down the hall, my toes tingling with the coldness rising up off the wooden floor. Approaching the kitchen, I saw a stain of light oozing out into the hall and at the same moment heard their voices. The skin on my chest and back and upper arms rippled with cold.

"Why the hell for?" my dad was saying. "For cryingoutloud ain't you got enough to do here?" His voice sounded funny, strained or stretched or something.

"Yes, of course. I can do everything that needs to be done here as well as this." It was one of my mom's voices, the one she used when she was angry with me or Kathy or Mary Ellen.

"Well who the hell's gonna do the cookin' and what about if one of them kids gets sick or somethin'? You ain't thoughta that, have ya. Them kids needs you 'round the house. One of 'em might get themselves killt or christknowswhat. All hell's gonna break lose."

"It's only two nights a week, Johnny, and it won't even start until September, so I really I don't think everything will fall apart. Kathy's seventeen and Del is old enough to take care of himself and both of them can look after Mary Ellen."

My dad was silent for a while and I could hear him breathing hard through his nose. I hugged myself and wiggled my toes to stop from shivering but I didn't dare move more than that. Then my dad spoke. "Well, shit I just don't understand. Ain't you happy with me?"

"Oh, don't be ridiculous. My going to night school two nights a week does not mean the end of our marriage." Then both were silent for a few long moments which were quiet and still enough to hear the clicking of the clock on top of the refrigerator. It seemed like an hour had gone by before my mom spoke out of the silence, "I deserve this."

"Hell, honey, I work like a sonofabitch for you guys, bust my ass to give you everythin' you need, and I don't see no call for you to be runnin' off like a crazy woman just to sit in a classroom. Hell, you got enough books here, ain'tcha?"

"It's not only the books, Johnny. You can learn a lot from a good teacher like the ones they have down at the community college."

"They're all a bunch of crazy bastards down there anyways. Bunch of crooks and egg heads." To this my mom clicked her tongue loudly but remained silent in the face of the on-coming lecture.

"When I was a kid there weren't no need for a wife and a mother to go runnin' off to school. Why my mother used to tell us..."

My lips were trembling violently and my toes were numb, so I drew in a deep breath, held it and, pivoting on one foot, turned round and crept back down the hall and slunk into my room. After silently closing the door, I jumped into bed, pulled the covers over my head and melted dreamily in the sudden delightful warmth. Foggily, I passed in and out of sleep, awaking again at just after eight. Sitting up in bed, I opened and closed my mouth several times fast to make a sticky slapping sound as I turned to look at Davy. He was on his back and holding my sock up at arm's length, blinking at it.

"Let's get up, fathead. Daylight's a-burning." I had heard that in a Western movie.

"This was on my forehead."

"You hungry?"

"I think it's one of yours. Smells like it."

"Stop screwin' around. Let's get up."

While we were eating granola in the kitchen, my mom passed through carrying a basket of laundry. She was frowning and her eyes were dark. I told her that Davy and I were going to hike in the hills and would be gone all day and would it be alright to make some sandwiches and bring a bottle of orange juice and all she said was "Yes, OK," as she was leaving the room. So we slurped down the rest of the milk from our bowls and we made sandwiches of bread and salami and tomatoes with a thin spread of mayonnaise and sweet brown mustard on the bread slices. We wrapped the sandwiches in plastic wrap and put them into Davy's army surplus bag along with two apples and a bottle of orange juice. I went back to my room to get the BB gun and my pocketknife and then we set out.

"Can I carry the BB gun?" asked Davy.

"No."

"Why come?"

"'Cause you don't know how to carry a gun and you'll probably shoot my eyeball out."

"Aw c'mon. Lemmie carry for a little while. I brought the magazines."

I thought over this angle for a second, then handed Davy the gun saying, "Carry it like this, with the barrel pointing at the ground, or with two hands like this so it points off into the bushes. If you ever point it at me I'll hate you forever and I won't ever invite you up here again."

"Alright. Here." Davy slipped out of the backpack and passed it over to me. I wove my arms through the pack's straps and hoisted it up, feeling its weight settle into the space between my shoulders.

Walking past the pole barn, we stopped to have a look at Taffy's box. She was in there with her swollen belly, rolled tightly into a doughnut and when she heard our boots scraping roughly against the red rock of the driveway, she lifted her head and stared at us with empty, brown eyes, sniffed our scents, and then laid her head back down again.

We left her, crawled over the wooden fence, then down the weed-covered slope and up again climbing a large hill. Duke emerged from the earth and ran along with us, but I stopped and pointed down the hill. "Go home, Duke. Go home." The dog looked at me with his ears pricked, pink rubbery tongue dangling. "Go home. You can't come with us." Duke just sat on the ground and watched me, his head at an angle. The warm intelligence in his eyes told me that he understood every word I was saying. Finally, I stooped and pretended to pick up a stone and raised my arm to throw it at him. Duke sprang up and ran quickly downhill, towards the house. Then he stopped, turned and started to come up to us again. I repeated the threat and he walked briskly away.

We continued up the hill, then passed over its flattened top and strode easily along a deer path. Already you could see that the true summer was nearly here because the earth was powdery and dry and when you kicked at the ground little puffs of brown rose up into the air and hung there momentarily before drifting away. The grass was drying to a yellowish green, but stalks of miner's lettuce still had white flowers which sprang out of fragile green cups, and wild lilac waved at us with tiny satin hands of violet, blue and white. Fat marshmallow clouds hung sedated in the sky and the air was alive with the scents of chaparral and dying grass and drying flowers and sun-toasted ground.

Slicing through the scrub, the path twisted along its course, dropping down into shallow depressions in the land or climbing over smaller or larger hills, until it vanished into a small grassy pasture. Here we sat on an old fallen tree, crusted with drying moss and rotting away into dust, and ate the sandwiches and drank from the jar of orange juice. I set up some sticks a few yards away from the dead tree and we shot at them with the BB gun. As I reloaded, Davy grabbed my arm and said, "Hey, look." Following his extended arm, I saw a cottontail feeding on something just outside of the line of the chaparral. Its fur was a thick, lush brown which coruscated in the bright sunshine. Davy grabbed the rifle and raised it. I yanked it out of his hands.

"Hey, whatcha doin', Del?!"

"Don't shoot at 'im, just watch, dickhead. He's not hurtin' anybody. Besides, this old BB gun can't kill anythin' except maybe a bird, and half the time the BB just bounces of them and they fly off. You gotta have a real gun to hunt, dummy."

"I know that."

"Shuddup. Now, see. He's gone. Your loud mouth scared 'im off. C'mon, day light's a-burnin'." I stood up, shouldering the backpack.

"Quit sayin', 'a-burnin'.' It sounds stupid and besides you got it from a dumb cowboy movie."

"So?"

"So there."

"Race ya to the bush."

Without another word Davy shot off, with me panting hard on his back, arms working, feet thumping on the soft earth in the warming summer's air, laughing and sweating and pouring all my energy towards the growing wall of chaparral.

"First!" yelled Davy. "Ha-ha, beatcha!"

"With a head start," I gasped, trying to catch my breath. We walked along the edge of the bush until we found a gap and we turned into it. Here the deer trail was smooth and well-traveled and I pointed out deer and quail tracks and rabbit droppings to Davy as we hiked up a tall hill, dropped down into a shallow bowl in the earth, then up another, smaller hill which leveled off into a broad, grassy, gently declining slope. Half way down the slope we stopped and finished off the orange juice which was frothy from jiggling in the pack on my back, and sun-warmed. I pointed with the bottle.

"See that house right down there?"

"Yup."

"That's it."

"Where's the tepee?"

"In the back. C'mon." We jogged the rest of the way down the incline to the house which was surrounded by a dried out and peeling white picket fence that leaned and sagged and was missing several pickets. The house itself was unpainted redwood, turned gray with age, with a gable, two large French windows and a big oak door. We opened the crooked front gate and stepped into the yard, well kept but not immaculate which gave it a warm, used feeling. It was filled with twisted shapes of welded wrought iron, formed into daisies and worms, flying pigs and a laughing crocodile.

"This place is weird," said Davy. "What is all this junk?"

"They're sculptures. Ritchie Lane makes 'em when he's sick of makin' music and stuff."

"Who's Ritchie Lane?"

"The rock star guy, bozo."

We walked up the sagging wooden stairs to the front door and I pushed it open, laying the BB gun up against the wall. The door was never locked. Inside it was dark and we moved slowly along a wood paneled corridor towards a bar of light which spread itself out along the floor, revealing the fine red-brown parquet. The corridor flowed into a spacious living room with plush white throw rugs on the floor, large cushions studded with rainbows of Oriental beads and three electric and two acoustic guitars leaning against the wall. There were two big black amps, and a black piano as well. Light flooded in from the sliding glass doors at the back of the room.

"Nobody's home."

"Naw, he's probably out back. He doesn't live in the house; he calls it his studio. He lives in the tepee. "

"Wow," said Davy.

Passing through the glass doors, we stepped out into the dazzling sunlight again to find ourselves in the back yard, a spacious area thickly covered by rose plants and white and yellow African daisies. The tepee was set up under the shade of a large and leafy avocado tree. We moved over to it and I pushed back the flap.

"Hey hey whaddayya say," said Ritchie Lane. "It's Little Boy Turner and his faithful friend Tonto." Ritchie and a woman I'd never seen before laughed. They were leaning on cushions, their legs stretched out before them. The air smelt funny inside the tepee, not tobacco funny but a burning rope kind of smell. "Sit down my most groovy and outta sight cats." Ritchie's voice was smooth and easy, like running water and his eyes, as usual, were red and glassy. My dad told me he probably never got enough sleep and I guessed it was pretty hard to do so when you were a rock star making albums and stuff.

"Hi Ritchie," I said, "I hope we're not like buttin' in on you guys or nothin'. This is my friend Davy from the town. He's spendin' the night."

"Outta sight. This here's Morning Star, dig?" Morning Star nodded her head at us and smiled, a beautiful glowing smile. She had twinkling light brown eyes, a broad nose and full lips and dark, very straight long hair, under which you could see large dangly gold earrings. "How ya'll doin'?" she said sweetly. I couldn't stop my eyes from traveling from her face to her cut-off jeans and down her long, slender legs to her bare feet. I swallowed hard.

"Fine," I said, my voice cracking slightly.

"Where you get that fine hair of yours, child?"

I shrugged. "From my parents, I guess."

"I sure hope so man," laughed Ritchie.

"Let me feel that stuff. Mmm hmm. Softly golden locks. My moma'd kill for that." I liked how Morning Star stroked my hair and I liked her voice and the warmth in her eyes. Nobody had ever admired my curly hair before. Most of the kids at school called me lion head or fuzzy top and made stupid jokes like Gee, I guess you stuck your hand in a light socket, huh? or, Did you get scared real bad when you were a baby? and I never laughed. But I never cried, either.

"Watch out man, I think she likes you," said Ritchie to me.

I blushed. "Naw," said Morning Star. "I ain't goin' after no jail bait. I'm gonna hafta wait a few years for you, sugar." I didn't know what she was telling me, but it sounded nice so I blushed some more.

Davy was craning his head all over the place, his mouth open. "This is way neat. You guys really live here?"

"Yeah, man. I can't live in a square house. The circular shape's the groovy thing, man. It's where it's at if you wanna get in touch with the Mother of Nature and the old Indian grooves."

"Indians?" I said.

"Used to live all over these parts, man, 'til the white man came and killed 'em all off. But they didn't kill the spirit, dig? Couldn't kill the

52

spirit."

"You're an Injun, aren't ya?" asked Davy, looking at Ritchie Lane's long braided black hair, thin angular face and sharp nose. The glass beads he wore at his neck and the leather moccasins completed the image.

"Tryin' to be, man," said Ritchie. "I'm a-tryin' to be."

"I wanna be an Injun, too," grinned Davy.

"Then you better stop callin' 'em Injuns and call 'em Indians like is correct, honey," said Morning Star.

"Yeah, baby, and then you gotta grow your hair out, trash the sneakers for a pair of mocs and get your mamma to buy yourself some glass beads and a headband. Then you can come live with me and Morning Star in the tepee on the sacred burial grounds."

"Jeepers, that'd be great, huh Del?"

"Sure would."

"'Jeepers?'" laughed Morning Star sweetly. "People still actually be talkin' like that?"

"Certain tribes do," said Ritchie and both of them fell into a fit of prolonged giggling. When they recovered I said,

"Hey Ritchie, why don't you show us somethin' on your electric guitar?"

"Groovy idea, man. I could do with some tunes." We all stood up and went inside to the big music room where we sat down on the rugs and cushions on the floor. Ritchie picked up a red electric guitar and stuck one end of a cable into the back of it and the other end into an amp. He brushed his hand across the strings and a great *boaw* boomed out. Leaning over the instrument, he adjusted a couple of knobs on the body. Morning Star was sitting next to me and from the corners of my eyes I watched how she moved her elegant hands, each fingernail painted a different color--purple, red, orange, green, gold--brushing hair out of her eyes with airy grace and sitting with her long legs folded up under herself, big thighs curvaceous and smooth. Her perfume was flowery and light and slightly sweet. I drank it in.

"Whaddaya wanna hear?" asked Ritchie.

"Somethin' good," I said.

"Somethin' from the *Monkees*," suggested Davy, but Ritchie had already started the first bars of *House of the Rising Sun*. He didn't sing, but played it in a harder and louder and bigger sound than I had ever heard before. Eyes closed, head swaying back and forth, long braided hair dropping straight down, Ritchie Lane's face took on a relaxed but at the same time deep and thoughtful expression of intense concentration as the riffs filled up the room, resonating off the wooden walls. Morning Star leaned back on her arms with her eyes closed and a smile on her face. "Do it baby, do it," she murmured as if in a trance. Her earrings swayed magically. The chords, full of might and force, echoed deep down in my chest and I felt lifted up by a light, flying, sensation.

As Ritchie played, a young girl stepped quietly into the room. She had Morning Star's nose, but her eyes where smaller and darker and her hair short and curly. She was thin and lithe in her tie-dyed t-shirt and worn jeans, and had on sandals and tiny silver star-shaped earrings. She moved very lightly but deliberately across the room and sat down next to me, cross-legged.

"Hi," she said through the roar of electric images.

"Hi," I said. Then we both turned to watch Ritchie Lane's playing, his fingers dancing now up the neck of the guitar, now hitting the high soaring notes near the pickup. The room shook and fluttered as it filled with music. With a flurry of screaming, rushing power that yanked you up by the shirt collar and left you hanging in mid-air for an epoch of seconds, suddenly you were hurtled earthwards and landed with a *thump* on the wooden fool again. Then, silence, but a silence that was still pregnant with what had been there before. Giant bells clanged in my ears and my heart beat like I had just sprinted a hundred yards.

Davy crawled over to me and pulled on my shirttail.

"We goin' now?" he whispered

"No." The front of my head buzzed as if it had been stuck hard by a velvet-wrapped hammer.

"I don't like it. It's too loud and noisy and they're freaky."

"I think it's great."

"I wanna go."

"Well, I don't," I said. "I wanna hear some more."

"Well go ahead," said Davy standing up. "I'm gonna go shoot the

BB gun."

"OK. I'll come get you later." Davy got up and walked out of the room.

"What's the matter with your friend?" said the girl. Her voice was friendly and pretty, like her face.

"I dunno. Music's too loud for 'im I guess." Electrified notes still rang inside my skull.

"What's your name?"

"Del."

"I'm Rhonda. But you can call me Ronni, like everybody does." She flicked her chin at Morning Star. "That's my big sister, Bernadine."

"Bernadine? I thought her name was Morning Star."

Ronni rolled her eyes. "That's what she's calling herself, but in our family she's still Bernadine."

"Oh. You guys are new out here, aren'tcha? Where do you live?"

"We're both from back east, Detroit. There's riots over there now. But Bernadine moved out here last year and this summer I asked my momma to let me come out here for a visit and she said OK, so here I am. You want some gum?"

"Thanks," I said. The tips of our fingers brushed slightly as she handed me a stick, and something I had never felt before, something like nausea or terror or wonderment or desire or cold, cold fear, rose up fiery and icy and flickered for a moment inside my stomach. The gum exploded sweet and giving in my mouth and in an instant this feeling was gone. My brain still throbbed from the music.

"Ain't that boy got just the finest hair, girl?" Morning Star had turned towards us, smiling.

Ronni shook her head. "Mmm hmm," she said as I felt my ears burning.

"Why look at that, the boy's blushin'. What's a-matter, hon, ain't no girl never told how fine you look?"

My face was in flames. "No," I choked out.

Morning Star and Ritchie laughed, but Ronni smiled warmly at me as I considered jumping up and dashing out of the room. But the look on Ronni's face made me feel better.

"She's only messing with you, Del. She doesn't mean any harm."

"Yeah, I know. It's alright. I think you two are the nicest girls I ever met. Most of the girls at school are stupid and goofy and everybody makes fun of my hair and 'cause I'm skinny and stuff. But you guys don't do that."

"I know what you mean," said Ronni and she opened her mouth to say something more but suddenly there was a huge *bau wau bau* thundering as Ritchie Lane's guitar roared once more with sound. Turning our heads to watch him, I was startled to notice that that funny feeling was in my stomach again--and it felt sort of good.

That, Ritchie told us when he had finished, was a song called the *Burning of the Midnight Lamp* by some guy I had never heard of. Then he did some *Kinks* and another *Animals'* song. But by that time I saw how the floor was becoming streaked by long slashes of shadow and I knew it was time to start heading back home. I choose a break in the music to stand up. My head was swimming in the flood of chords and notes.

"Splittin' already, man?"

"Yeah Ritchie. I better get goin' or my dad'll throw a fit if I come home too late."

"Too bad, man, the jam's just beginnin'."

"All y'all ain't hungry?" asked Morning Star.

"No," I lied.

"Hush. Here, let me find you somethin' in the kitchen so y'all can munch on your way back." Before I could say don't worry about it, Morning Star was up and out of the room. Ronni was standing, too, with her feet placed close together. She was looking at them and smoothing down her t-shirt. Morning Star re-entered and handed me a couple of doughnuts and two bananas. "Here ya go, sugar. That oughta hold you and your friend."

"Gee, thanks. That's really nice of you."

"'Gee,'" laughed Morning Star, shaking her head. "Get outta town with your 'gee.' And she laughed some more.

Ritchie Lane was laughing too. "Man, that's Star's way of sayin' you're square."

I laughed along with them, although and didn't know at what. It wasn't a mean laughter so I didn't feel like a dummy for not knowing.

"Well, bye till next time," I said, walking to the front door.

"Keep cool, man."

"Bye, sugar."

Ronni followed me into the hall. "I'll walk you out," she said. We stepped out onto the front porch together, Ronni keeping one hand on the opened door. "Bye, Del," she said, stepping into the door frame, sunlight glancing down and throwing silky beams of gold onto her forehead and into her eyes.

"Yeah, bye. Maybe I'll see ya around sometime." My voice had suddenly grown weak and small and my head still rung from the music.

"Oh, yes. That'd be nice."

"Yeah." I shoved my hands into my pockets then took them out. "So, see ya later."

"Bye, Del. Come back soon."

"I will," I said, walking backwards. Then I waved, spun around and ran up the hill a short distance. When I turned around, she was no longer there, the closed door splashed with gold. Then I remembered Davy. There was a large boulder near by and I climbed up it and had a look around. Davy was off to the side of Ritchie Lane's house, crouched down and aiming the BB gun into the bush. I jumped down from the stone and carefully and quietly stole up on Davy, keeping behind him and watching the ground in front of me least I stepped on a brittle twig that would give me away. When I was quite near to him, I rushed forward yelling "*raaahh!*"

Davy screamed and sprang into the air, hitting the ground running. "Ha! Scared ya!"

Davy stopped and came towards me, panting, his face white. "Did not."

"Oh, don't even try it Davy. You jumped a mile in the sky."

"So?"

"So it's gettin' late. We'd better hit the trail." We started up the hill again, heading home.

"Took you long enough in there," said Davy as we walked side by side. "I thought you'd never come out."

"Ritchie Lane was playin' music."

"You call that music? Sounded like a cat barfin'."

"Shuddup. I thought it was really neat. I never heard a guitar make those weird sounds before."

"It gave me a headache. Who were those girls?"

"Dunno. First time I've seen 'em."

"They're ugly."

"Are not."

"Are too."

"I think they're two of the most prettiest girls I've ever seen."

"What?" said Davy, eyebrows arching. "But they're *black*."

"So what?"

"So they're ugly that's what's so what. All niggers are ugly and stupid."

"I told you not to say that word."

"We're not at your house and I can say what I like. It's a free country."

"Shuddup anyway. You're just an ignorant dumbshit."

"Your dad said that word last night so I guess he's ignorant, too, huh?"

"Yeah, that's right. So shuddup about sayin' it."

"You're just a nigger lover," grinned Davy at the same instant rushing down the trail at full speed. A shot of rage coursed through me and I tore after him, but he had too much of a head start and I couldn't catch him. From the protection of distance Davy called me that name again. I dropped my head and bent my arms like I was going to rush him, then stopped instantly and laughed when he took off running again. "Ha-ha faked you out, scaredy-cat!" I taunted, bending to pick up a large rock. When Davy turned to look at me, I hurled it at him. "Missed!" he yelled and I chased him again down the winding deer trail, the brittle green arms of the chaparral clawing my forearms, feet *thump-thump-thumping* the dried earth into powder, boiling blood throbbing in my head where veins swelled and strained and the sweat broke out under my arms and on my temples with Davy's teasing, fleeting form just visible through eyes blurred with the image of my fist crashing down on his mouth, my pale hands around his throat.

"I'll kill 'im," I kept saying to myself. "I'll kill 'im, I'll kill 'im, I'll kill 'im."

5

I chased Davy all the way home. I didn't want him to reach the sanctuary of our house before I could bash his face in, but he always stayed just a few yards ahead of me. As we descended the last hill leading down to my home, I suddenly rushed at him, straining with the last shreds of energy in my leg muscles, my chest aching as my arms pumped, propelling me forward. Again he had a good lead on me, but his foot caught on a root sticking up from the ground and he stumbled but did not fall. It was enough to close the gap and a hot shot of adrenaline pulsed through me as I closed the space between us to a couple of feet just as we scurried under the wooden fence and burst across the driveway, my arm stretched forward, yearning fingers spidering out inches away from Davy's back, legs thrusting me onward with a last blast of energy, and fingers at last closing around the back of Davy's shirt collar. I yanked with all my might and he fell, with me tumbling on top of him. After a quick scuffle, I got his head in an arm lock and squeezed.

"Take it back," I panted, my face buzzing red, eyes stinging with rage and salt.

"Ow! Cut it out! Take what back?"

"Take it back what you said back there." I squeezed harder.

"Ow! Hey, that hurts."

"Say you're sorry."

"Lemmie up, lemmie up." Davy dug his feet into the ground and rammed his shoulder into my stomach, at the same time groping upwards with a hand. Fingers slashed my face.

"Ow!" I said, punching him in his side.

Suddenly I felt hands, other hands, pulling on my shoulder. "Stop it!" said my mother's voice. "You stop this nonsense this instant."

I let go of Davy and he rolled away from me. I stood up, fists curled into hard little balls at my side.

"What's the meaning of this?" demanded my mother.

I pointed. "He started it."

"Never did," said Davy, rubbing his neck.

"Shut up."

"You shut up."

"Make me."

"Both of you stop it now," said my mother firmly, stepping in between us. "Davy, go to Del's room right this minute and don't come out until I say." Davy glared at me, then turned sullenly and walked away. When he was gone, my mom looked at me. Her face was pale and her lips tight. "I'm sick of this idiocy," she said, her voice a terrible whispered tremble. "This whole family's mad and I've got to watch the whole crazy bunch of you and I've had it up to here."

I stared at her. "Don't you even want to hear my side?"

"No. Go to your room."

"I can't. You sent Davy there."

My mom's eyes slashed at me. "Go pull weeds. For godsakes I've been asking you to do that for a week now and at least you could help me out sometimes. Everything's always on me in this house, isn't it? Go," she pointed, biting the inside of her lower lip. "Go do some work around here for once."

I let out an angry *pppffff* sound and stomped off towards the back yard where I sulked around the daisies and rose bushes, my hands in my pockets, occasionally kicking a mud clod or a weed with the toe of my boot. They could beat me or ground me or not let me watch TV for a week, and I still wasn't going to do it: there was no way that I was going to pull weeds, no matter what. I crushed a weed under my heel, but it sprang right back up again. What a stupid place to live, I thought. My dad's a wild man, the Monster's a brat, Davy's a jerk, Kathy is always mean and my mom's always pissed off at something. I felt like running back into the hills, all the way over to Ritchie Lane's place again where I could be with Ronni and her big sister and they'd say nice things to me and we'd listen to Ritchie playing and sit in the tepee and eat doughnuts and crack jokes.

But it was hard to stay mad on such a perfect summer's day. The back yard was full of tiny white butterflies and large orange Monarchs with black lacey patterns etched on their frail wings. They were attracted by the light perfume of the flowers which rose up to hang in the air while high above fat bellowing puffs of white and gray chased each other across the late afternoon blue. Very shortly, my bad mood was gone and I left the yard and entered the living room through the sliding glass door. As I stepped in the shadowed and cool room, I caught sight of my mom, sitting on the sofa with a book. I froze, and the idea flashed across my brain that I should turn and run, but I figured she already knew I was standing there, so I crossed over and slumped down into the big chair.

"Whatcha readin'?"

My mom did not look up. "A book."

"It ain't right if you're still mad at me."

"'Isn't.' And you know how I feel about fighting in this house."

"We were fightin' outside."

My mom looked at me over her book. "Don't get smart, Del."

"Davy made me mad."

"I don't care, you're not supposed to fight. Think of your hero Bobby Kennedy. He's against fighting."

"Alright, but what are you supposed to do when someone calls you a bad name? Just shut up and take it?"

"Reason with them. You're not a child anymore."

"Some people you can't reason with, like daddy."

My mom finished the sentence she was reading and closed the book on her finger. "Your father is a special case. I know how to deal with him. What did Davy say to you?"

"He called me a nigger lover."

My mom's face darkened and I saw a jaw muscle twitch. "Well, the next time that boy says something like that, you tell him he is crude and ignorant."

"I did."

"And if he says it again, he'll have to come and speak to me."

"Good. I'll tell 'im that. That'll shut 'im up." I glanced down at the book on her lap. "So whatcha readin' anyways?"

My mom gazed at the book in her lap as if someone had secretly laid it there while she was looking somewhere else. "Oh, just some poetry."

"Yuck. We gotta read that junk in school."

"That's good. You should read more."

"Why? It's boring and stupid and nobody likes it. Nobody understands it."

"It's not boring," said my mom, her eyes lightening up, "and it certainly isn't stupid. Stupidly read, but very rarely stupidly written. The best of it is uplifting, it adds something extra to your life, lets you escape from..." my mom's eyes roved around the room and I had the feeling there was a word lying tucked away in some corner that she needed "...from so many things. Everyday things. And sometimes you're not supposed to understand what a poem says."

"Huh?"

"Sometimes it's just a collection of rhymes and images to produce a special feeling inside you. Like this one," she opened her book, thumbed through a couple of pages and read. When she finished she closed the book again and looked up at me. "Well?" she asked. "What did you think of that?"

I shrugged. "I guess it's an acquired taste. Maybe you gotta read a lot. Mom, why do you read so much all the time?"

"I don't read 'all the time.' I don't have enough time to read half the things I'd like to."

"But you're always readin' if you ask me. The Mon--I mean, Mary Ellen--can't read 'cause she's so young and Kathy's always out with her friends and daddy only looks at the newspaper sometimes and I got my comic books and stuff, but you're always readin' big books with hard backs and no pictures, most times about some famous old dead guy from history like Napoleon or Oscar Wilde or Byron. Why come?"

My mom sighed like she was tired, then looked at me, then off outside the sliding glass door, and finally back to me again. "I guess it's for the same reason I like poetry and some people like the movies or watching TV or cars or like you with your model planes. It's just a way to remove yourself from things."

"You mean like playin'?" I asked, and then added, "But it's not like playin' 'cause the people back then were so stuffy and stiff like." I picked up a large, heavy book from off the coffee table and flipped through it, glancing at the faded black and white photos of tall narrow houses with ornate facades and big doors, and square-headed men with handle bar moustaches, thick eyebrows and high starched collars, and thin-lipped gray-faced women who wore their hair in tight buns and had enormous bosoms and puffy white dresses. Holding up an opened page of the book, I said, "What a screwy time."

"It wasn't a 'screwy time,'" said my mom, "it was an elegant, cultured and graceful time."

"Their clothes were too tight."

"That's because they were specially cut for them by highly skilled tailors. Silk, velvet, trimmings of gold and silver: they wore only the finest materials back then. Oh, what a gracious, sparkling age."

I was going to say something like no way, but I noticed that my mom was looking outside again. With a slow, steady gaze she seemed to be picking something out of the summer's air. Her hands were still, but her head and the living dreaming eyes glowing out of her head moved in half-time, taking in light and once more giving me the impression of her not really being here, not really sitting on drawn up legs on the couch in the living room, and that she was outside, far away outside, somewhere away from the chaparral hills and dirt roads and corrals and houses and out of this our present time. But with a short intake of breath, she suddenly snapped back. "Well," she said brightly, "I'd better clean up the kitchen. Kay Lifton-Wright and her daughter are coming over."

"What, now?"

My mom nodded. "Oh, no," I moaned, "that alky?"

"Don't say that Del. It's not nice. If you must use a description then you can at least say alcoholic, which is the correct term."

64

"But she is an alky. Everybody knows it. You can always smell it on her and her eyes are funny looking."

"Well, she has her problems. She's divorced, you know and she's trying to deal with so many things."

"But she's got loads of money. That should make her happy enough."

"That never makes you happy. And besides, she doesn't have as much money as most people believe. She's not so well off."

"Well, she sure acts rich. Do I gotta hang out with her daughter?"

"Why not? Don't you like Wanda? She likes you, you know."

"Yuck," I said.

"Well, just try to be civil to them, and for godsakes don't stare."

"But Kay's eyes are so creepy lookin'."

"Just don't stare, Del, and try to put yourself in her shoes."

"I'd wear sunglasses."

"She has problems. She has to work them out in her own way."

"Whatever," I said, getting up. "I'm gonna go see what Davy's up to. He better not be messin' with things in my room or I'll..." my mom was looking at me "...I'll tell on him to his mom."

I crept up to my room on the tips of my toes, holding my breath. Reaching my closed door, I gently pressed my ear against it, listening for the soft sounds of Davy crushing my models or ripping pages out of my favorite comics. Silence. With a swift, fluid movement, I turned the doorknob and stepped inside. Davy was crouched down on the floor, his hands hidden, the glossy pink sheen of an open magazine on the floor in front of him. Acting as if I hadn't seen anything, I went straight to my bed and flopped down on it. I could hear Davy standing up and the simultaneous zip of his jeans and a metallic snap.

"Why don't you get outta here?" he said.

"It's my room. You get out."

"No."

"Get out."

"No."

"Then shuddup."

"You shuddup."

We were both silent, and in the silence the air grew heavy and thick. From the rasp of Davy's jeans I knew he had sat back down. Then there was a brittle rustling.

"Don't touch my models," I said to the wall.

"I'm working on my own if you must know, mush brain."

"Oh." Swinging my legs up and over, I did a backwards summersault and rolled off the bed onto the sweaty stickiness of the beanbag. My head spun round and the rush of blood made my face and ears throb with heat. Davy didn't even look up.

"I bet you couldn'ta done that," I said with menace.

"I wouldn't want to."

"Just don't say that word anymore, Davy."

The fine plastic pieces turned slowly in Davy's hand. In the other he held his hobby knife and he bent to slice a part off its sprue. "I won't," he said. "Not in your house."

"Alright."

"Alright."

I crawled across the floor to get my model and sat working alongside Davy. "We got guests comin' over," I said, "and we gotta talk with the lady's daughter when they come."

"Rats."

"Yeah, I know but if we don't my mom'll get mad at us and she'll make us work in the yard pullin' weeds and stuff."

"Nah-uh. It's not my house. I don't gotta pull weeds."

"Then she'll call your mom and you'll hafta go home."

"Rats," said Davy, and we were silent for a while, working on our kits.

An hour later, I pushed my kit away from me and leaned back on my elbows. "Let's go outside now Davy. You wanna play Secret Service for Bobby again?"

Davy opened his mouth to answer, then looked at the bedroom window. "Hey," he said, "I think there's someone comin'."

I turned my head toward the outside wall, listening. "It's them," I said, standing up and going to the window. Down below on the dirt road, Kay's white Chevrolet emerged from a cloud of yellow dust. "Yup. Here they come. Let's wait in here and maybe we can sneak out later and not hafta talk to 'em."

"Yeah."

Crouched near the bedroom door, we heard the car roll up onto the driveway, the dull damp sounds of doors closing followed by muffled voices. Then, surprisingly clear and loud, my mom called out "Del!" Looking at Davy, I placed a raised index finger to my pursed lips, turned the doorknob and eased it shut. I jerked my thumb at the floor and whispered, "C'mon. Let's keep playin' like we didn't hear anythin'." Davy nodded, and picked up a comic book as I knelt down over my model kit.

Scarcely had I done so, when there was the light sound of approaching footsteps, the knob rattled and the door swung open. "Can I come in." It was not a question.

"No."

Already inside, Wanda walked over to my bed and sat down. She was wearing a shapeless light blue dress with flowers printed on it and it clung damply to her flat chest and boyish hips. Her thin yellow hair, looking wet or greasy, clung to her scalp and a lock of it was pulled back behind her ear and held in place by a red plastic barrette. Her arms and legs were thin and pale and so was her face. No eyebrows and no eyelashes hung over her light blue depthless eyes and her aquiline nose led down to thin gray lips. "Whatcha doin'?" she asked.

"What's it look like."

"You still play, Del?" she said, "You're too old for that now aren't you?"

I didn't answer.

"I'm already fourteen and I got a boyfriend at school and his name's Carl and my mom lets me go to dances with him. We go to dances and he's sixteen and learning how to drive." I glanced up at Wanda, sitting on my bed with her bony legs slightly apart. She had on shiny black patent leather shoes and white socks that barely covered her ankles. "And Carl and I go to the movies sometimes," Wanda continued, "the matinee, and one time he drove me around in his mom's car. I gave all my horses and Barbies to my little sister. Mom says next year I can wear lipstick if I want. Then I'll be in high school."

"So?"

"So when are you goin' to high school?"

"I don't know. I'm in no rush."

"You gotta girlfriend?" asked Wanda, twisting the word girlfriend out into a sort of taunt or challenge or demand.

"Nope," I said. "And I don't want one."

"And your friend there?" Wanda flicked her chin at Davy, whose face was covered by the comic book.

"He doesn't want one neither."

"What's a-matter with 'im, cat got his tongue or somethin'?"

"No," said Davy from behind the comic book.

"What's a-matter, you gotta scar or somethin' so you gotta hide your face all the time?"

Davy sighed and closed the comic. Rising to his feet he said to me, "I gotta take a whiz," and left the room.

"What a weirdo," said Wanda, watching him go. "He a friend of yours?"

"No. A complete stranger. Never seen him before."

"That's pretty funny," said Wanda, not laughing. "Carl's funny and he's a good dancer, too. You like to dance, Del?"

"Never tried."

Wanda stood up, arms spread away from her body. She spun round in a tight circle until the hem of her dress lifted and floated up just like a dancing woman in a Hollywood musical. "You oughta not play with toys anymore, Del. Stand up and I'll show you how to dance like I do with Carl."

I was about to tell her to shut up and get out of my room and that I didn't play with toys anymore anyways, but then I remembered that my mom asked me to try to be nice to her. With a groan I got to my feet and stood near Wanda. She came closer to me.

"Here," she said, "look. You gotta lift your feet like this and then turn and move your arms just like they do on Dick Clark or the *Monkees*."

Watching Wanda dance, I tried to copy her movements, feeling awkward and stupid. My feet weighed a ton and it seemed my arms were stiff with hardened plaster. Then I stopped. "I can't do it like you."

"Sure you can. It's just hard now 'cause we don't have any music. I know what we can do," Wanda said stepping up close to me, "we can slow dance. It's easier to do and you don't gotta have music either." Nearly the same height as me, she stood with her toes up against mine, then took both of my hands in hers.

"Hey," I said. Wanda's hands were cold and sweaty.

"It's slow dancing. This is the way you do it, just like on TV." She pressed her body right up next to mine. "Now," she said, "you're supposed to put your one hand down here --" I gulped: one part of my hand was on her hip, the other resting on her butt "--and the other pressed across my back and then we kinda of sway back and forth, back and forth. Relax, Del, your body's as stiff as a board. Can't dance if you don't relax."

Wanda placed her head on my shoulder and clasped her arms tightly around my waist, squeezing. Her hair smelled musty and I could feel the bones protruding from under her thin dress. Then in one quick movement she lifted her head, pushed her open mouth towards me and put her tongue into my mouth.

"*Plaaah!*" I said, pushing her away from me. I spat on the floor and wiped my mouth several times on my shirt sleeve. "Oh, gross out. *Plaaah*. Whaddaya tryin' to do?"

"Just showin' what Carl and I do."

"That's *not* dancin'."

Wanda put her hands on her hips and shook her head. "Oh, c'mon Del. You're not a baby any more. Grow up. Geez."

"Del! Del!" I looked at the doorway to my room. "C'mere," said the Monster. "Taffy's dyin'!"

I pushed past Wanda and followed the Monster down the hall. Passing by the bathroom, I banged on the door. "I'm outside, Davy," I yelled and I heard the muffled reply, "OK. I'm comin'," and the toilet flushed. The Monster was holding my hand, and I allowed her to pull me into the kitchen. My mom sat with Kay Lifton-Wright at the table and when we entered the room, she looked up at us. "Del," said my mom, "say hello to Kay."

"Hi."

"Good day," Kay said, nodding to me. She looked more shrunken than the last time I had seen her, and yet puffy, too. Although she was a couple years younger than my mom, she appeared ten years older. The skin on her face and arms was loose and flabby and her hands shook. You could see that once it had been a fine face, but now it was ravaged. Tiny purple veins x-ed her nose and her lips stood out, too full and too red for the rest of the receding face. She was drinking from a milk container, the waxed cardboard kind you get at the school cafeteria, with a straw sticking out of it, and there was no milk in it. Everybody knew that it was vodka and orange juice. I didn't want to look up into her eyes, but my gaze was drawn there as it always was. They were red and watery and the dull, lightless pupils swam in a squishiness that made me want to barf. They weren't living eyes, but some gooey plastic creation of a mad doctor with frizzy hair and a thick accent from a *Hammer* horror film. I dropped my gaze and looked at my mom. "Mary Ellen says there's something the matter with Taffy. I better go'n have a look."

"C'mon," said Mary Ellen, tugging on my hand. We walked outside into the fading sunlight and crossed the driveway to the pole barn.

Davy came up and stood next to us as we looked at Taffy in her box. She was panting heavily and her whole body trembled with each gulp of air she sucked in. Her stomach was big and swollen and a light pink color and there were a couple of rows of small, stiff nipples strung across it and hair sprinkled here and there over the stretched skin. Soft and pink and wet, her tongue lolled out of her mouth. Taffy watched us with brown expressionless eyes, blinking rarely.

"She's dyin', Del," said Mary Ellen. "Is she dyin'?"

"Looks like she doesn't want to eat nothin'," said Davy. "Look at her dish. It's full."

"We gotta make her eat," said Mary Ellen, squatting down near the dog. Picking up a piece of the dried, day-old dog food, she offered it to Taffy. The dog didn't even sniff at it, but merely closed her mouth and swallowed and resumed panting again.

I scratched my head. "Well, Mary Ellen. If she was hungry, I guess she'd eat so it's no good tryin' to force her. Maybe the way she's actin' means that the puppies are coming, huh Davy?"

"Beats me."

70

Mary Ellen looked up at me, smiling. "Oh, boy. The puppies are comin'!"

"I'm not sure now, Mary Ellen. We should ask daddy when he gets home."

"The puppies, the puppies! Daddy says I get to have one for my very own and I'm goin' to name 'im a secret name."

"Ask me if I care," said Davy. "You'll probably give 'im a goofy girl name like Flower or Peaches or Mumphy-Mumphy."

"And it's gonna be my very own little baby and I'm gonna be its mother," said Mary Ellen. "Oh boy, the puppies are comin'!"

There was an engine roar and the front end of my dad's pickup suddenly reared up over the incline leading to our house, then the entire truck rolled into view. The motor cut off and all at once everything was deathly still and silent. I could see the back of my dad's head and his thick grizzled neck. Nothing stirred, not even the breeze. My dad gave out a long sigh, almost a moan. Slowly, the door creaked open and my dad, just like he did six days a week, stepped out of the cab, slammed the door shut with a *boom!* and marched heavily into the house, his steel lunch box in one hand, an old coat slung over his shoulder. We watched him wordlessly, transfixed.

"Daddy's home," I said at last.

6

Mary Ellen took off at top speed after my dad. I put my head down and had to run full out to catch her.

"Lemmie go, lemmie go!" she screamed, arms flailing and legs kicking. Her entire compact, tiny body was a rubbery twisting worm of frantic energy. "Lemmie go Del, I wanna tell daddy!"

I pinned Mary Ellen against my chest and carried her back to the pole barn. "We'll tell daddy later, goofball. Don't do it now, he'll just yell at you. You know how he is when he first comes home."

Gradually, she stopped squirming in my arms and I set her down on the ground again, watchful, ready to spring if she made another rush for the house. "C'mon," I said, "let's play tag."

Mary Ellen smiled and pointed her finger. "You're it."

"Wellll... OK!" I suddenly said, chasing after Davy and the Monster, who screamed with delight. My arm extended in front of me, I went after Mary Ellen, making wide sweeps with my hand which always just missed her by inches. She loved it, and giggled and squealed in excitement. While we were playing, a red Ford pickup drove up the driveway and I stopped running. The bed was filled with girls and as the truck came to a halt, Kathy crawled down from their midst and waved goodbye, then walked up to the driver's side and spoke to a blonde boy in the cab. He laughed, gunned the engine and the truck rolled back down the hill. Kathy watched it go out of sight, then turned towards us. She had on a one-piece green-and-yellow striped bathing suit, and sandals and held a rolled up towel in one hand. She walked over to us.

"Hi," she said, and then to me, "Did daddy just get home?"

"Yeah. Couple minutes ago." Kathy's hair was still wet and it hung long and dark and limp from her head. She smelled like coconut. "Were you at the beach?"

"The lake. Did you see what kind of mood he's in?"

"Nope. But Kay Lifton-Wright's here with her weirdo daughter so he's probably alright. Besides, you haven't done anythin' wrong this time for him to get mad, right?"

"No. We were just at the lake," Kathy said, almost defensively. "Mom knew where I was."

"You know dad. He just likes to have everybody around the house all the time or he worries."

"I know," said Kathy. "It makes me sick."

Mary Ellen pushed forward and hugged Kathy's leg and Kathy rubbed her head. "Taffy's babies' comin' soon."

"Is that right?" said Kathy. "Let's see."

Mary Ellen showed Kathy the dog, then Kathy stooped to pick up her little sister and carried her into the house, Mary Ellen held almost as a living shield in Kathy's arms. This was an often-successful ploy that I knew quite well.

"That's your big sister, huh?" asked Davy as both girls vanished inside.

"No duh."

"She's kinda pretty."

"Pretty dumb."

"How come?"

"'Cause she's always fightin' with my parents about all kinds of stupid stuff."

"So what? I still think she's pretty."

"Forget it, she's already gotta boyfriend and besides she'd never be interested in a goofy shrimp like you."

"Bet you she'd like my big brother, especially if she saw him in his uniform. Talk about love at first sight."

"More likely fight at first sight. There'd be like this major battle between her boyfriend and your brother."

"Yeah, that'd be neato."

"Yeah," I agreed, and then added, "C'mon, let's go inside, too." My stomach muscles tightened as I braced myself for another family battle.

In the kitchen, surprisingly, everybody was laughing. I let out a happy sigh. My mom sat at the table next to my dad who was in his chair holding Mary Ellen on his lap. An empty plate with streaks of grease on it was in front of him and he was drinking a gin tonic. Kay was sitting opposite my dad posed like some kind of a model and Wanda stood behind her, thin and pale and blue in a shadowed corner of the room. She smiled at me as Davy and I entered, shifted her weight from one foot to the other and put a finger in her mouth.

"Dinner's on the stove," said my mom.

Davy and I went to the cupboard, took down plates and got forks from the drawer and then opened a big pot on the burner. With a large wooden spoon, I served Davy and myself. It was spaghetti with pine nuts, fresh tomatoes and pesto sauce. My mom had also made a baguette, which was glistening with garlic and olive oil, sprinkled with parsley and parmesan cheese.

"It's really neat eating at your place," said Davy as we sat down at the table. "Gosh, I never had green spaghetti before. The bread is super yummy."

My dad was making himself another gin. "Kay," he asked, "want some of this?"

"Oh, no Johnny, I've think I've had quite enough thank you. Don't want to overdo it, you know."

"Alright," smiled my dad, twisting in his seat to put the bottle back into the glass cabinet.

"But," said Kay, patting the back of her head with a hand, "if you insist, I do believe I will have just a drop."

My dad poured the gin and topped it off with tonic water. Kay watched my dad fixing the drink like a hungry dog watches someone eating a t-bone steak. "Don't forget the lemon," said Kay, "or the ice. One cube, please."

"There ya go, Kay. That'll put hair on your chest."

Davy burst out in a laugh, bits of spaghetti and pesto splattering his plate and a surrounding ring of table. I giggled, too. My mom rolled her eyes.

"Oh, Johnny," said Kay, "you are so terribly earthy."

"Simply charming," said my mom.

"Hell yes," grinned my dad. "'I'm a ding dong daddy from Yuma, you oughta see me strut my stuff.' 'Member that corny old tune?"

Kay raised her glass. "And a poet, too." I forgot not to look and so I saw her eyes again. Red eggs in yellow yogurt, rubbery, mushy and slick. I instantly dropped my gaze and stared at the table for several long seconds before I could continue eating.

Kay drained her drink and set it delicately on the table. "Well," she said. "I do believe it's getting to be rather late. Wanda?"

"Right behind you, mother," said a voice from the shadows.

"Are you ready? I think it's time we get a move on."

"Hittin' the high road already, Kay? Hell, you can stay longer if ya like, you don't gotta run off."

"Thank you, but we really must be going. I've got a tea on tomorrow and I need my beauty rest."

"She better make it a long one," Davy whispered to me. I shoveled a mound of noodles into my mouth to stifle it as my chest shook with silent laughter.

Kay and Wanda walked to the front door with my mom and dad close behind them. I turned in my chair to watch them go and just then Wanda whipped her head around and smiled at me with her thin, gray lips. "Bye, Del," she said, and skipped out of the room.

When they were gone, my dad sat back down in his seat. "That crazy bitch," he said. "I can't stand a drunk woman. That Kay ain't got no class."

My mom was at the sink, filling the coffee kettle. "Well then why do you always treat her like she's royalty?"

"She oughta take some care of herself. She looks like hell."

"You shouldn't ply her with drinks that way, and maybe she'd go sooner." My mom came to the table with two mugs in her hand.

"Well, hell, honey, what the hell kinda host do ya think I am?"

"I certainly hope she makes it home alright. She really shouldn't drive in such a state. But you can never reason with her. She won't even admit that she drinks too much."

"Drunks never get hurt in a crash anywho. They're too damn rubbery and relaxed. They just flop all over the place and go to sleep and never known what the hell hit 'im."

"But Wanda. She could be hurt, you know."

"Ah, they'll be alright. Kay's never crashed a car in all the years you known her. She's got that dumb drunk's luck. Ain't that right, ya little critter?" My dad held Mary Ellen up in the air and shook her until her face turned tomato red and the laughter tinkled out of her opened mouth. He set her down on his lap.

"Daddy, know what?"

"What?"

"Taffy's gonna have babies soon."

"Well, hell I know that Mary Ellen."

"No," I said, swallowing a mouthful, "She means real soon. Taffy's acting all strange and stuff."

"Hey, lemmie tell it," said Mary Ellen. "Taffy don't eat--"

"'Won't,'" inserted my mom.

"Won't eat and don't wanna drink and she just sits in the box and does this all the time." The Monster stuck her tongue out and panted.

"Well I'll be damned," said my dad. "I think maybe we oughta go have a look see. Could be them puppies is comin' tonight alright." My dad rose up from the table like a Sequoia, and strode forward, we kids trotting after him into the purple lengthening shadows and went over to where Taffy still lay in her box. She was resting on her side, her distended belly rising and falling as she laboriously drew in short breaths, her neck stretched out and her eyes closed.

My dad watched her for several minutes, and then bent down and stroked her head. "Sonofabitch," he said thoughtfully. "Tonight just might be the night, alright."

"Wow!" said Mary Ellen in a whisper. "Puppies."

"This old box ain't gonna do for them pups, though," said my dad, rubbing his chin. "I think I fix her up a real dog house. Del? You and your friend there go round back and get me a sheet of plywood. I'm gonna build the S.O.B. right now. Get goin'."

Davy and I ran around the back of the barn to the wood pile and picked up a plywood sheet from a stack, taking a corner in each hand. When we brought it round front, my dad had turned the barn's fluorescent lights on and set up two wooden saw horses. With one hand he grasped hold of the plywood and slapped it down on the horses. "Plug this in, boy," he said to Davy, giving him one end of a cord which snaked out of an electric saw. My dad looked at me. "Del, stop standin' around with your finger up your ass and go get me a hammer and some nails." I jumped to it, going into the small tool room with its grease stained floor, fluorescent lights and big, broad work table crowded with chisels, dies, drill bits, files and wood planes and about a hundred other things. Bending under the table I pulled out a box of nails, stood up and took a claw hammer off the table. Then I carried it all out to my dad who stood holding the electric saw in one hand, eyeing down the sheet of plywood. He put the saw on the wood, pressed the button and the jagged teeth ripped through the wood in seconds, sending up a fine spray of saw dust into the air. Davy sneezed. My dad set the saw down and stood a section of the cut wood on end. "Give me a hand here," he growled, "and set them nails and hammer over here." He glanced at the nail box I was carrying. "Not them goddamn nails for cryingoutloud!" he exploded. "Them's sixteen-penny roofing nails. Jesus H. Christ, bring me them eight-penny construction ones, Del, you know the ones I mean, damn it. Christ almighty!" Swallowing hard, I ran back into the tool room, dragged out another box of nails and presented them to my dad, praying silently that they were the correct ones. He didn't scream at me and I let out a long, low sigh of relief. Davy was holding a sheet of cut plywood end up and looking at my dad with big eyes. I could see his Adam's apple wobbling in his throat.

With a couple of skillful, deft motions, the sides of the doghouse went up. My dad cut some more wood and hammered the pieces together and tacked a small gabled roof on top of that. Then he stood back with his meaty fists on his hips and admired the thing. "Lookin' good, eh boys? I think we all did a pretty damn good job of it. Whaddaya say, Del?"

"Looks great, dad." I could feel myself swelling a little with pride. I was happy whenever my dad was happy, especially because it was such a rare occurrence. I turned my head and smiled at Davy who beamed back at me. Then my dad opened his arms wide, bent at his knees, hugged the sides of the dog house and heaved the entire thing up and carried it over to Taffy's box. The dog didn't even look up as the house hovered over her head and then was carefully lowered down.

"There ya go, Taffy girl," said my dad. "Your own little mansion." He winked at me.

"Hey Taffy," said the Monster, sitting on her haunches and peering into the doghouse.

"Leave her be," said my dad. "She don't wanna be bothered right now. She's got a hard time aheada her. C'mon now, let's get in. It's getting chiller than hell out here."

We followed my dad's tree trunk frame back to the kitchen, me bending my head and snuggling my hands into my pants' pockets because of an evening breeze which swept low and cool along the driveway as it came in off the Pacific ocean miles away, making the dried grass rustle and sigh and setting dead leaves to chatter. Opening the kitchen door, we stepped right into the middle of an intense conversation between my mom and Kathy, which cut off abruptly as we all entered. My dad, after a staring pause, dropped like a sack of feed into his chair. He looked first at my mom, then Kathy, then back to my mom, rubbing his large hands over themselves, over calluses, cracked skin, busted fingers.

"What're you two yakkin' about?" he said.

My mom glared at Kathy who was wearing a white skirt that came up to her thighs, a tight black turtleneck, fishnet stockings and white patent leather shoes with high heels.

"Kathy has plans to go out tonight," said my mom in her mom voice.

"Where to?"

My mom looked over at Kathy and Kathy said, "A concert."

"Who with?"

"Ernie."

"Ernie Porter?"

Kathy nodded.

"What kinda concert?"

"A music concert."

"I ain't no fool."

Kathy shifted the weight off one foot and onto another. "OK, a rock concert."

My dad laughed a short laugh which was really a snort. "The hell you are."

"Mom!" said Kathy, turning towards my mom.

"Not dressed like that you ain't."

"I told you, Kathleen," said my mom through her teeth.

Kathy spoke to my mom. "But all the girls dress this way and their parents let them."

"You ain't old enough to go out thataways," said my dad.

"Maureen Carter," said Kathy, still only addressing my mom, "she wears miniskirts up to here and white go-go boots and its OK. It's not fair that I have to wear these ungroovy fuddy-duddy clothes like some sort of weirdo country bumpkin."

"Sarah, tell that girl that she ain't goin' out dressed like that."

"I have told her, John," retorted my mom firmly.

Kathy stamped her thick high heel on the floor. "You *have to* let me go out. I'm not a baby anymore. I'm nearly eighteen-years-old. You can't treat me this way."

"Sarah, tell her she--"

"You tell her, John," said my mom, eyes flashing, bared teeth white and sharp and small in her head.

"I can't talk to these kids. Nobody listens to me."

My mom faced Kathy. "Listen, you're not going out like that, that's final. When you're 18, alright, but when you're still living under this roof, you'll dress decently. Go change and you can go to your concert. But not like that."

"Looks like a goddamned whore," muttered my dad.

"You're all dictators!" said Kathy, eyes red and watering. "I can't believe how you're ruinin' my life!"

"Tell her to go change," said my dad to my mom.

"Change and you can go out. That's it."

"No! I won't change. I'm not going to the concert. You've ruined everythin', you've screwed up my whole life," sobbed Kathy, tears streaming down from hot angry eyes. "I hate living here!" she screamed, running off to her bedroom.

"Goddamned kids don't never listen to me," grumbled my dad loudly, "Ain't no daughter of mine goin' out lookin' like a whore. I know how these young fellers are. I know what's goin' through their heads alright and she ain't goin' out there lookin' like that, god damn it. Sarah, you gotta talk to these kids sometimes, make 'em understand they can't just go runnin' all over hell like goddamned chickens with their heads pulled off."

My mother was leaning against the kitchen counter, arms folded, eyes glowing hot and hard. "I do talk with them. I'm the only one who talks with them. I'm always the middle person." Her voice was low and measured.

"Weren't never this way when I was a kid. No siree, when my mom said to jump you jumped or you got the shit beat outta ya. Hell, my old man used to wait for me to come home and then he start wailin' on me..." I kicked Davy in the ankle and started easing into the hallway "...he wouldn't just stand there talkin' with ya, he'd lay in with both goddamned fists, boy, and I'd just cover up my head and roll into a ball and take it, him just wailin' away, beatin' on me for all he's worth..."

Davy, Mary Ellen and I were out in the hall now, walking fast. When we got to the living room, I switched on the TV and we sat on the floor, our backs resting up against the sofa. Mary Ellen rested her head on my arm.

"See what I mean about Kathy?" I said, eyes staring dully at the faintly glimmering screen. "She's dumb."

"How come dumb?"

"She's always gotta try and take on my parents. It never works that way."

Davy nodded. "Yup. Just makes 'em sore at you."

"Yeah," I said slowly, my brain's gray matter being sucked into the magical singing box, "It's never a fair fight. The parents always win."

Davy's mouth was hanging open, his face flickering blue. "Uh-huh," he mumbled.

"You gotta outsmart 'em," I said, but no one was listening. The commercials were over and there was someone speaking to us rapidly out of the TV, and laughter. We kids poured our eyes into it.

Several minutes later my mom walked into the room, a large hardback in one hand, and from her gait and the way she swung her arms, I could tell she was still angry. "Turn it down," snapped the unopened mouth with the sharp teeth. I turned it down. My mom settled into a corner of the sofa, drawing her knees up with the open book resting on them, her head plunged deep inside. Shortly after that I heard the stomp of my dad. Entering, he commanded, "Switch on the news and turn it up," and sank into his chair. I did as told, quickly, then sidled over to where Davy sat just as my dad stretched out his massive legs, his feet still shod in his heavy work boots. The war was the opening story, as it had been for as long as I could remember. The reporter said that the fighting was heavy and many Americans had been killed and wounded and many South Vietnamese but much more VC, so we were still winning. Davy and I both sat up when they showed clips of helicopters firing machine guns into the jungle, and then an explosion, white and airy, from an air strike and then pictures of three VC prisoners, sitting in a row on the ground. Their mouths were open and they squinted up at the camera and their hands were bound behind their backs and they had no shoes. Helmeted men in black boots and green pants with rifles with bayonets attached stood behind them, looking bored.

"I bet they're Marines that got 'em," said Davy enthusiastically.

"Yeah. I'll bet your brother was in on it," I said, moving my legs into a more comfortable position. I looked down at Mary Ellen, who was fast asleep.

"Yeah. He's always where the action is."

Then, as always, there was footage of a demonstration against the war in some big city back east. The TV showed us a small army of policemen in helmets with clear Plexiglas face guards and blue shirts and with billy clubs in their hands forming up into a line and then rushing the demonstrators, clubs swinging.

"Will ya look at that," said my dad, "Poor bastards. Them goddamn cops don't mess around, boy. I hate them sonsabitches."

"That mean you're for the peace marchers, dad?"

"Shit on 'em, too, Del. They're all a bunch of crazy nuts."

Following this were the political stories. They showed Bobby first, small and gray and sad and lost looking in a huge pulsating sea of people, all grabbing out at him. When he smiled, his eyes crinkled up and though he was smiling, you could see the melancholy just dripping off his hunched shoulders.

"There's Bobby, mom."

"Mmm hmm," came from behind me.

"Hey," I said, "RFK's here in California."

"It's the primary, bozo," said Davy with disdain.

"Oh. Hey, he's in L.A.! Bobby's in L.A., mom. Gosh, I wish I was there. "You votin' in the primary, dad?"

"Hell no. They're all a bunch of crooks. I ain't votin'. It's all rigged anyways. I don't trust the bastards no how. Look what they done to JFK."

"You, mom?"

"It's too late now, Del," said my mom, watching the screen. "I didn't vote because all the polls say RFK will win California."

"Yeah!" I said. "But you're gonna vote for president, aren'tcha?"

"Of course," said my mom, returning her gaze to her book when the cramped, sneering face of Nixon filled the screen.

"Good ole Tricky Dick," said my dad. "There's a dirty crooked bastard for ya alright." Feeling that another tirade was about to begin, I stood up and motioned to Davy, whispering, "C'mon, let's go outside and have a look see if the puppies are here yet," just as my dad cleared his throat. "Sonofabitchin' politicians just ain't the same no more. Franklin Delano Roosevelt, now there was a hell of a man for ya. He was for the regular Joe Blow in the street. He weren't crooked like all them nowadays."

"Did you vote for him?" asked my mom, reading. Davy and I stepped into the hallway.

"Hell no, I ain't never vote. Good ole FDR. It was he started up all them programs. You had you your CCC and the WPA and then there was the..."

Davy and I left my dad's voice and stories and mumbled memories back in the house. We were outside now and it was cold. I could feel tiny silver fish slithering along my forearms and down my back, causing my skin to tremble from the chill. With short, brisk steps we crossed the driveway to Tafffy's new doghouse. I bent over and peeked inside.

"Hey Taffy girl."

Davy rapped his knuckles on the doghouse's wooden roof.

"Cut it out, butthead," I said to him. "Don't bother her."

"Why not? I'm just wakin' her up a little."

"We shouldn't bug her 'cause then she'll get upset and nervous and stuff and when the puppies come she'll freak out and eat 'em."

"Since when are you the puppy expert? How do you know all this stuff?"

"I read it in a book."

"What book?"

"Let's go back inside," I said, shivering and rubbing my hands up and down my arms. "I'm freezin'."

"Race ya back," said Davy.

"Well..." I said, standing up and facing the front door. Suddenly I bolted, my whole body instantly transformed into a warm, elastic beast of movement and speed, egged on with the sound of Davy's pounding feet in my ears. "First!" I yelled laughingly as I slapped the front door with the palm of my hand.

"Cheater."

"Loser."

We went into my bedroom, me springing onto the bed, Davy dropping into the beanbag.

"Know what?"

"What?"

"That's what."

"Shuddup."

"No really," said Davy, "know what we oughta do?"

"Yes."

"We oughta stay up all night long. That way we can be there when the puppies come and we'll be the first to see it."

"Yeah," I said, sitting up. "And then we can hear about if RFK won the primary or not. But we gotta be kinda quiet or my dad'll yell at us."

Davy nodded and, still sitting in the beanbag, used his feet to drag himself across the floor to his model kit. I slipped out of bed and started working on my airplane again.

We worked steadily and quietly for a couple of hours. I painted the inside of the fuselage and glued the halves together and attached the lower wing as well. The night outside my window was very black but clear and pure looking, a clear mountain night's sky that always means cold. The black was as deep and rich as bitter chocolate, but the stars, hard and stony and icy, lay like a thin silver screen beyond or perhaps just in front of the dark. Shortly after eleven o'clock, I looked over at Davy, saying, "I think I'll go out and take a look at how's Taffy doin'."

"No, I'll go," said Davy, "I'm tired of sittin'. I wanna stretch my legs." Taking one of my windbreakers, he left and I stared out into the starry night.

Davy returned after ten minutes or so, his cheeks flushed and his eyes wide. "Boy," he said excitedly, "the puppies are here and you missed it, Del!

My mouth dropped open. "What?" I jumped to my feet.

Davy collapsed laughing into the beanbag. "Faked you out."

"Dickhead," I said, not laughing and sitting back down. "How is she doin' really?"

"OK. Looks the same. Your dad was out at the doghouse, too, just watchin' her. He said he's always hated waitin' round for babies to come. He said he'll come and get us when they start comin'."

"What about the primaries?"

Davy had picked up a part of his tank and was examining it. "Who cares?" he shrugged.

We worked on our kits, talked and looked at comic books until after midnight. Although it was late, I did not feel at all tired. The night seemed full of something alive, crouching in the shadows, a tense, rustling presence in the evening breeze, a certain expectancy in the air as if it were filled with firecrackers waiting to go off. Then I heard footsteps in the hall, heavy and familiar, and a second later there was a knock on my bedroom door and at the same time the handle turned. My dad's head appeared. "Boys," he said. "It's started."

Davy and I sprang up and walked at a fast pace with my dad to the pole barn. My dad held a flashlight in one hand and its beam shone out like a glimmering rod, carving rough shapes out of the night. The serrated tread of a truck's tire. The solid geometry of stacked chips of wood. The crude fanged edges of large stones. When we got to Taffy's house, my dad covered the flashlight's ray with his hand so that only a soft reddish glow came out, barely illuminating the inside of the dog house.

"Take a look see," he said.

Davy and I pressed our heads together as we stared into the cutaway door. Taffy lay on her side, her body arched into a half-circle. Two pale, wet, sticky things looking like living gym socks or large worms, nestled, shifted and squirmed near her belly and Taffy put her muzzle down to sniff them. Then she licked her babies. Davy and I stood stock still in the night at the dog house, watching in open-mouthed amazement as the other puppies emerged from their mother, eyes tightly shut, frail, slick bodies trembling in the evening air, faces all scrunched up like an old man's.

"Ain't that a hell of thing to see, boys?" said my dad.

"Wow wee," whispered Davy. I could only nod.

As we stood there watching, I heard the crunch of footsteps behind me. Straightening up and turning around, I saw a black shape cut out from the surrounding blackness approaching. As the form grew near, I could just make out my mom's nose and high forehead.

"Come to see the pups, Sarah?" my dad asked.

My mom walked right up to my dad and put her arms around him. When she spoke her voice sounded high and taut. I didn't know this voice. "Oh, Johnny," she said in such a tone so that I knew instantly that she had been crying. "They just shot Bobby Kennedy."

7

"Sonofabitch," said my dad. "What the hell happened?"

With one hand, my mom wiped the tears away from her eyes. Speaking rapidly in a weird, strained voice she told us how RFK had just won in California and North Dakota and he was in the Ambassador Hotel in L.A. saying something about going on to Chicago and he gave the victory sign, stepped off the platform and went into some back room and then it happened, and my mom started crying again as my dad held her in his big arms.

"Christ," he said softly, as I just stood there staring at my mom's shaking shoulders, mouth open, mind numb, eyes registering dark, floating, smudged images that my brain could not process. I remember putting my hand to my mouth and saying "Oh no." Then I was watching the huddled indistinct forms of my parents receding towards the house and my feet somehow stumbled forward, following. Davy was at my side.

"Jeepers. All those Kennedys get it," he said. "My mom says they got a curse on 'em. Bad luck and stuff and that she wouldn't wanna be one of them for all the gold in the world. She says they got somethin' about 'em that makes people not like 'em and makes 'em want to kill 'em and so she says if you ever have one of 'em comin' to your town you shouldn't go to see 'em 'cause there's sure to be some shootin' goin' on."

I didn't turn to look at Davy. "Shuddup," was all I said. I could feel

Davy staring at me, but he did not say anything more, except,
"Jeez."

Without feeling the floor underneath my feet or my hands hanging limp at my sides, dead of touch and sight and sound, I shuffled woodenly into my bedroom, mechanically switched off the light, and dropped into my bed, face down. Then it hit, a great wave rising up out of the pit of my stomach which gushed out of my throat in an anguished sob. In an unthinking daze, I cried until my throat hurt and my chest felt exhausted, until at last, fitfully, I passed into sleep.

I almost woke up happy in the morning. Rested and alert, I heard the birds singing to themselves outside my window and could see that it was going to be another beautiful day. But quickly the memory of last night returned, although I played a game within myself whereby what I had seen had not been real but a dream, a bad joke, a late night horror film on TV. But with the rising sun and the yawning of the great blue summer's sky, I knew. The daylight showed me it was true.

Lying on my back, I stared up at the ceiling, so wide and broad, a horizonless blank of white. From his breathing and certain rustling noises, I knew that Davy was already up. I didn't say anything to him, though, I just kept my eyes fixed straight ahead.

There was a punch on my shoulder. I my eyes bored into the ceiling.

"Hey, aren'tcha gettin' up? I'm leaving today. My mom'll be here any minute."

I was silent.

"Hey, Del. What's a-matter? You sick or somethin'?" I turned to look at Davy, who was standing off to one side, running a thin black comb through his hair. "My mom'll kill me if my hair's messed up. You gonna get up?"

I tried to say "yes", but my voice only came out as a hoarse whisper. I cleared my throat and said it louder, then swung my feet off the bed onto the floor. My head felt thick and I had the sensation that my eyes had grown large, round and bulbous in the night. They stung.

"Boy, do you look bad. I guess you got the flu or somethin'. Did you like get up and barf last night?" Davy didn't wait for my answer, which I wouldn't have given him anyways. "I thought I heard someone late in the night like throwin' up in the bathroom. You know those weird garglin' sounds?"

"Davy, shuddup."

Davy widened his eyes at me. "Hey, what gives? You still in a bad mood?"

"Yes."

"Well you shouldn't take it out on people who haven't done nothin' to you."

I pushed past him, went to the bathroom and splashed cold water on my face. I tried to pat my frizzed hair down, but it kept springing up. In the mirror, I caught a real glimpse of my face, but I didn't hold the image in my head and I quickly dropped my eyes. I could feel how my face must look; I didn't need to see it. Leaving the bathroom, I realized for the first time that I had slept fully clothed.

Davy was already in the kitchen, eating a bowl of granola with banana sliced into it, and two pieces of toast. I poured myself a glass of apple juice and sat down just as my mom stepped in with a load of laundry in her hands. Her face was ashen and she hadn't brushed her hair either. I didn't look at her eyes because I didn't need to. I knew what they looked like. Nobody spoke. The only sound was Davy's chopping on the toast and slurping his granola from his spoon. It sounded especially loud in the big, white kitchen.

I glared at him. "Hasn't anyone ever told you you should shut your trap when you eat?"

Davy smacked his lips at me. "Stop bein' in a bad mood. You're no fun anymore."

I gripped my glass and raised it slowly to my lips, looking at Davy over the rim. If my mom hadn't been in the room, I would have thrown it into his stupid, cheery face.

Then Duke started barking and there was the noise of a motor ticking over. "That's your mom," I said. "Thank god."

My mom, Davy and I went outside. Davy's mom sat in the station wagon, an arm resting on the rolled down window. She tilted one cheek out the window and Davy dutifully walked over and planted a kiss on it. Then he got into the passenger seat.

"Terrible news today, isn't it Mrs. Turner?"

"Yes," said my mom.

"Hubris is what I call it Mrs. Turner, although George says it's comeuppance. You know, for arrogance, that sort of thing. That family's had it coming for a long time."

"I wouldn't agree with that," said my mom, her voice held low and tight.

"Well, whatever. But it is a shame to see it happen like this. Who knows what this country's coming to. I certainly hope my David behaved himself."

"He was fine."

"They're wild at this age, you know. You've got to keep an eye on them every minute," said Mrs. Peterson, talking about her son as if he were not a part of her own living self but was some form of domestic plant or lower animal life. "They'll run you ragged if you let them."

Neither my mom nor I had anything to say.

"Well," said Davy's mom. "I've got a busy day ahead of me, as I'm sure you do, too, so I won't keep you any longer. David, did you thank your hosts?"

"Thanks, I mean, thank you, Mrs. Turner," Then he turned to me. "See ya later."

"Bye," I said gloomily.

"A good day to you," said Mrs. Peterson with a short nod of her head, and she put the car into reverse and they were gone.

My mom and I stood there for a silent moment. It was a clear, cloudless morning, the air still edged with a slight chill, and there was a mild breeze coming out from the west.

"Is he dead?" I croaked. It hurt to swallow.

"Not yet," said my mom. "He's in the hospital and they're operating on him. But everyone says there's no hope." She sighed with a deep weariness. "There never seems to be any hope." And she went inside.

Duke trotted up to me where I stood and I squatted down and stroked his head and chest. He pushed his warm wet muzzle into my face, nudging me, and licked my cheek. Sitting down Indian style, I pet Duke for a long time, just sitting there close along side his living warmth, feeling the slow butter of the growing sun seeping into my dazed head, smelling Duke's particular odor, the earth scents rising up from the ground, a sharp tinge of chaparral carried on the wispy breeze. Could people really die in the summer? I wondered. How could the sun, the glowing strength and power of the long golden days, allow it? I stopped rubbing Duke's chest and through my fingertips felt the slow regular beat within. Was it truly possible to die in the summertime?

After a while I stood up and went to have a look at Taffy. She had eaten her food and I refilled it from a bag in the barn, and put fresh water into her bowl. The puppies had already lost their worm-like appearance from the night before and where forming into the more recognizable shapes of dogs. They nursed happily from Taffy's belly, while she, content and relaxed, stretched out and closed her eyes. I ran my finger down the back on one pup that I had already chosen for myself, a black and white one with one black ear. It was so small and delicate and fuzzy that I couldn't help myself from smiling.

After this, I went over to the fence, crawled through it and set out for the horse barn across the pasture, with Duke following. The high grass was a pale green fading into brown at the tips and on the outer edges. Large, tan-colored grasshoppers sprang out of the way of my feet as I crunched forward. I came to the sight were the lizard had died, and picked up the stone that marked his grave. He was still there, but not a clean white skeleton yet. His little body was blackened by ants and empty holes that had once been eyes gaped out at me spookily. Duke took a sniff at him and I was afraid he was going to try to eat him, so I pushed his head away. Replacing the stone, we continued on our way to the barn.

I climbed up the wooden fence and sat on the top rail, facing the corral. The barn was quiet and it was strange to me that Smokey was not to be seen. Then I noticed that the tack room door was open so I hopped off the fence and walked around the barn to the water trough under the big oak tree where my sister stood, running a horse brush through Smokey's yellow mane.

"Hi," I said. Smokey snorted, lifted one hoof and looked at me from the side of his head. His nose skimming the ground, Duke trotted off into one of the stalls.

"Hi," said Kathy, brushing.

"Whatcha doin'?"

"Gettin' ready for a ride. What are you doin' out here so early?" said my sister, now stroking Smokey's massive back. "Where's your little friend?"

"He's gone home. Did ya hear what happened?

"About RFK? Yeah. Pretty rotten."

"Yeah," I said.

Kathy turned around at me, picking long yellow strands from the tightly clustered bristles of the brush. Smokey nudged her on the shoulder with is big snout. "Taffy had her puppies last night, didn't she?"

"Yeah. I thought about wakin' you up to tell you, but then I didn't."

"Good. I wouldn't have come out. I didn't want to see mom and dad."

"'Cause of the fight, huh?"

"Because of all the fights. I'm sick of them."

I walked up to Smokey and patted him on the rump. "Well, you gotta live with 'em somehow."

"Only for a year."

"Yeah, whatever. 'Til your 18. So why not try and put up with 'em 'til then? It's no use takin' on daddy 'cause he's a wild man and he always starts rantin' and ravin'. You oughta lay low and do what you wanna do without 'em catchin' on to what you're up to."

"No way. It doesn't work that way, Del. Not with mom anyway. She's so damn nosey. She's always askin' questions, snoopin' around, tryin' to figure out who are my friends and what we do together. It drives me crazy. And dad. Well, there's a definite generation gap there. He's out of it. His time was the '30's and 40's and he just can get into what's happenin' now. He's nowhere."

I rubbed my hand across Smokey's strong back and haunches, fingertips tingling with the sensation of the firm, awesome power pulsating deep within the muscles, tendons and bones, hot and violent with the blood of a wildness that would never be tamed. A sweet, distinctly horse smell filled my nostrils. "So what are you gonna do-- just keep on fightin' 'em all the time?"

Kathy took Smokey's head in both hands and looked at his face. "I don't know. Maybe split."

"Split? You mean like, run away?" My hand stopped rubbing the horse.

"Yeah, maybe. I can't deal with it here anymore. It's easier for you and Mary Ellen because you're both young. But me, I'm more grown up. I need my space, personal freedom. Mom and dad just don't understand that."

"Wow," I said. "Maybe you oughta think about it some more. I mean like where would you go, what would you do?"

"I'd be with Ernie, and maybe even a couple of friends from school. We could take Ernie's car and--" Kathy stopped, turned and stared hard at me--"you promise not to tell mom or daddy?"

"Yes."

"Promise."

"I promise on dead Aunt Louise's grave."

Kathy stared at me for a long second. "OK. You'd better keep it. So, we're thinkin' of takin' off in Ernie's car and goin' up north to San Francisco, the Haight or to the Berkeley scene. It's totally happenin' up there and there's all kinds of young people just hangin' out and groovin' together without any parents to bring you down."

"Boy. Mom and dad would freak."

"So let them. That's their problem if they can't deal. Do me a favor, Del. Go get my saddle and blanket. I want to ride while it's still mornin'."

I went into the tack room, immediately struck by the full smell of leather and rope and wool. The saddle was placed on a wooden horse my dad had made, the blanket draped near it. I threw the blanket over the saddle, grabbed it by the horn and yanked it off its mount and onto my thigh. In this way I carried it to Kathy. She had already fitted the bridle on and I handed her first the blanket and then the saddle; she put both onto the horse. The cinch pulled tight under Smokey's round belly, Kathy gripped the saddle horn, slipped her foot into the stirrup and swung a leg over the horse's back. Smokey stomped and shook his mane, working the bridle into his mouth.

"Open the gate for me, Del."

Running over to the gate which my dad had constructed out of welded scrap pipe metal, I undid the latch and swung it back wide enough to let horse and rider through. "Have fun," I called to my sister as she headed down the dirt road.

"See ya later," she yelled back, without turning around.

Just as I started to close the gate, Duke dashed out and caught up with my sister and I watched them all go off together until they disappeared behind a thick rise of bush.

I climbed up onto the fence again, straddled the topmost plank and looked out on our land: the wide pasture green turning to yellow to brown, the one-storey house sitting on a small flat-topped hill, the broad dusty driveway, the pole barn rising up from one end of it. I could see the yard and in the yard the clusters of white and yellow daisies, looking like fluffy little clouds skimming the surface of the earth. Swelling up behind the house was a hill and off to the side of the pole barn an even larger hill, thick with brittle, scratchy dark green chaparral. I could see no one, no living person or animal, no shivering cottontails or prehistoric lizards or elegant, gliding hawks. My sister was gone, and Smokey and Duke as well, and my dad was gone off to work; my mom was gone inside the house and with her Mary Ellen, and Davy was gone home. Bobby was gone now, too, or almost gone, and at this moment there was only me. Only me. Under the yawning vastness of the sky everything looked so small, and the land so empty and sad. I thought about what my sister had just said in the corral, and I thought about RFK, but then I didn't want to think about it anymore because the thoughts got me nowhere and only spun round and round inside my head in ever tighter circles. I felt like crying again, but I knew it would be the dry, heaving sobbing type of crying that comes up out of the bottom of your stomach and leaves such a terrible, hollow, raw feeling. So I jumped off the fence and into the grass growing out of the soft earth, crossed the pasture, and made for the big hill. Climbing it I didn't know where I wanted to go, if anywhere, but I knew I didn't want to cry anymore. Not just yet anyway. Then, in the walking up the hill, I realized where it was I was heading and that this, I felt, was the only possible direction to take. So I pressed on upwards.

8

Walking rapidly along the deer path which in slow, lazy convolutions wound through the surrounding bush, all my senses were finely tuned to the vibrant hum of early morning life teeming in the undergrowth. Dew clung to the grass like little diamonds. Birds called to one another in voices of pure music, fresh deer tracks and rabbit droppings petaled the way before me and lighter-than-air gray squirrels silently leapt between the tree branches, their pelts flashing silver in the sun. Seeing and hearing these things made me feel a little better, just as they helped to assure me that it was indeed still summer.

In what appeared to me to be a flash, I suddenly found myself standing on top of the grassy hill which sloped down to Ritchie Lane's place. I descended at a half trot, in the process stirring up a nest of butterflies in my stomach at the thought of seeing her again. When I reached the front yard, I decided not to go in through the house, but to cut around it. I was certain they'd all be in the tepee.

They were. When I entered, Ritchie Lane and Morning Star were sitting on cushions, Ritchie with an acoustic guitar in his hands which he was not playing. But Ronni was not there and my heart sank a little realizing this.

"Hey, baby," said Ritchie, "come on in."

"What's happenin'?" smiled Morning Star, eyes twinkling with warm intelligence. Today she was wearing a multi-colored headband, a loose lavender blouse that tied around the waist and buckskin pants which weren't normal pants at all but consisted of four pieces of laced-together soft leather with a space left between each half so that her smooth, firm skin was exposed. Ritchie Lane had on a purple-fringed vest and old jeans. Both were barefoot.

"Hi, you guys," I said, sitting down. The air in the tepee, as usual, smelled funny. "What's goin' on?"

"Not much. We were just groovin' to some tunes, man. Tryin' to drive away the blues, you know what I'm talkin' about?"

"Yeah," I nodded. "You mean about Bobby."

Morning Star shook her head. "Fucked up, man."

"That's how it is in the Land of Milk and Honey, babies."

"That's right," said Morning Star. "That's how it be. I'm tellin' you, they be takin' people like us out. You try and stand up for yourself, say your say like they done told us we could in school, and they'll take your ass out."

"Ain't even no use tryin' to go up against 'em."

"That's right," continued Morning Star. "You got it. First it was ole Medgar Evers gunned down before his own house, after that JFK, then they got Malcolm, and then Martin Luther. They took 'em all out."

"And now they got Bobby," said Ritchie Lane.

"Who's they?" I asked, confused.

"The establishment, man," said Ritchie.

Visions of clandestine para-military groups dressed in black tights with small pistols and plastic explosives and jagged-edged knives clenched in their mouths filled my mind. "Who's the establishment?"

Morning Star looked at me. "That's everybody, sugar."

"All the squares. It's your parents, man, and the teachers and politicians and bankers and the pigs and the military people."

I thought of my teachers at school down in the town and of Davy's mother, too. "Yeah, I guess I know some of them. There's a lot of 'em, aren't there?"

"Everywhere, man, everywhere you look. Squares and pigs are crawlin' all over the place." Ritchie had taken a bag of tobacco and some rolling papers from out of a leather pouch and was rolling a cigarette, just like in a cowboy movie.

"But they ain't got long," said Morning Star. "The Gentle People are takin' over."

"That's our last and only hope, man. A Freak revolution, a love happenin'. All the squares who hate are nowhere, man." Ritchie rolled the cigarette tightly, twisting the ends and sliding the whole thing between his pursed lips to seal it. Then he placed it in his mouth, lit it with a lighter and drew in a deep breath. The end of the cigarette glowed hotly. Ritchie passed it to Morning Star. "You wanna hit of that?" said Ritchie, his voice a high whisper.

"Naw, cigarettes make me cough. I tried one once in back of the bleachers at school and I didn't like it."

"This ain't no cigarette, man," squeaked Ritchie Lane.

"What's the matter with your voice?" I asked.

Laughter burst out of Ritchie's mouth, along with a stream of grayness. The smoke smelled funny to me, an aroma I had often noticed before in the tepee and inside the house.

"You're too much, sugar," laughed Morning Star. "You sure you ain't some kinda spy for the Feds or somethin'?"

"Ain't nothin' the matter with my voice, man. Its just like when you take a hit, you gotta keep the smoke in or you won't get high, dig?"

"Oh."

"Here," said Morning Star, "you wanna try some?"

I shrugged. "OK." I took the burning cigarette out of her hands and held it for a second, not really knowing what I should do with it.

"Look, man," Ritchie Lane instructed, "pinch it between your two fingers like this, then take a hit. And don't forget to hold in the smoke for as long as you can."

I did what he told me, my cheeks puffing out as they filled with smoke.

"Naw, don't do it that way," said Morning Star, "you gotta suck it on down into your lungs, see what I'm sayin'?"

I nodded, then swallowed, handing the cigarette to Ritchie as a silent fit of coughing shook my chest.

"Don't let it out, man," said Ritchie, taking a hit.

I nodded again and held my breath for as long as I could, and then a bit longer. When my lungs began to hurt, I exhaled a large gasp of air, watching with perplexed fascination as blue-gray smoke streamed out of my face. Then I sat there, opening and closing my mouth to get the taste and waiting for something to happen.

"Well?" asked Ritchie. "Whaddaya think? Can you feel it?"

I focused my eyes on the beadwork of a cushion and tried to concentrate on if I could feel anything different or not. After a couple of seconds, I glanced up at Ritchie saying, "I don't feel anythin'."

"You gots to take more hits, sugar," now Morning Star was speaking in a funny voice, "and also you gots to let yourself go. Get into it."

"Vibes, man. Pick up on the vibes. It's a love thing, baby."

"OK," I said.

Ritchie Lane leaned towards me. "Here, man, take another toke."

I did, held it for a long minute, then let it out slow and easy.

"The boy's a natural," laughed Morning Star.

I leaned back on a cushion feeling my head wobbling on my thin neck; I had the sensation that it was about to float right off the rest of my body and this made me smile. Morning Star was passing the cigarette back to Ritchie, but I took it out of her hand and put it into my mouth.

"This sure is a great cigarette," I said.

Morning Star and Ritchie laughed. "No, that ain't no cigarette, man. It's a joint."

"Mary Jane."

"California Gold, man. My old man called it 'Gage,' back in the day. Back in the '20's when he played sax in a jazz trio."

"I'm talkin' weed, sugar." Morning Star began giggling and watching her started me giggling, too, and Ritchie Lane as well. I laughed and laughed and then stopped suddenly, staring at Ritchie's vest. There were brightly colored spots all over it, yellow and red, blue and white and green. I blinked, looked again and crawled across the cushions to get a better view, and stuck out a hand to feel one. It was cold and smooth and flat. "Oh!" I said out loud to no one. "They're buttons." Reading them, I began laughing again. A small yellow one proclaimed *J. Edgar Hoover Sleeps with a Night Light*, another said *STOP You're Blowing My Mind* and a blue one with white lettering announced *WARNING: Your Local Police are Armed and Dangerous*. I read out loud the message on a green one: *My Button Loves Your Button*, and began giggling all over again.

"Man, you're trippin'," laughed Ritchie Lane.

"He's stoned," said Morning Star. I turned to look at her.

"And you're beautiful."

"Look out!" said Ritchie, "Oh, look out!"

"Boy, if Ronni hears that she'll be mader'n hell."

I sat up. "Ronni? Ronni. Hey, where's Ronni at anyways?"

"Inside the house, man. Groovin'."

"Far out," I said, not knowing what that meant and deciding at that moment to stand up and within that very moment watching myself from somewhere within myself deciding to stand up. So I stood up. "Bye-bye," I said, flinging the door flap to one side and with a raised straight leg and a perfectly vertical foot, stepped into the garden like some toy soldier. Behind me, floating out from inside the tepee, I heard guitar music. Marching stiffed-legged across the garden, I was acutely aware that I was walking across the garden, knowing with each step exactly where my foot would fall, which mud clods would explode under it, which blades of grass would bend and flatten. And then, without knowing how I had gotten there, I was in the music room, sitting on a large cushion and vaguely wondering where all the others had gone.

"Hi, Del," said a voice but not from inside my body. "Where'd you come from?"

I looked up. "Hey, Ronni."

She sat down next to me. "How did you get in here, Del? I didn't hear you come in."

My forehead wrinkled. "I was in the tepee, and then I was here. That's how."

Ronni was looking at me closely. "You've been smoking weed, haven't you?"

"Nope."

"Have too. My sister and Ritchie got you high, huh?"

"Uh-uh. I don't think so."

"Get outta here. I can tell from your eyes. And you got that smell all over you."

"Know what? I think you and your sister are the most beautiful women I've ever seen not in a magazine. I mean like in real life."

Ronni averted her eyes from mine. "Shut up, boy. You're talking trash now."

I lay back on a cushion, hands clasped behind my head. "This is a far out place. I like it here. Everythin's nice. You're lucky you can live here with Ritchie Lane and such a far out sister."

"Well, she's not always so far out. Sometimes she gets on my nerves. She tries to tell me what to do all the time and I don't like that. She ain't, I mean, she's not my momma. You got any sisters and brothers?"

"Two sisters, and I'm in the middle."

"What does your momma do?"

I shrugged. "Cook. Clean up, the shoppin'. But mostly she reads. She's readin' all the time. She doesn't go anywhere without a book in her hand."

"I'm that way, too," said Ronni. She was sitting cross-legged and looking at me with her big, serious eyes. "I love books. I wanna be a teacher so I can work all the time with books. Bernadine calls me the bookworm, says I'm gonna have to get glasses if I don't quit. She says I'll burn my eyes out."

"That's not true. My mom don't wear glasses and she reads more than anybody I know."

"Doesn't."

"What?" I said.

"You said, 'My mom don't' and it's supposed to be 'My mom doesn't'."

"Boy, you're just like my mom. You oughta meet her."

"I'd liked to."

"OK. Next time maybe. What's your dad do?"

Ronni's face darkened and her eyes grew hard. She looked down at the floor. "He's gone."

"Where to?"

"I don't know. He's just gone. Run off somewhere. Maybe to New York, maybe down south somewhere where he's got family. Nobody knows."

"My big sister wants to run away from home," I said, almost as if I were proud of it.

"Why?"

"'Cause she fights all the time with my dad and mom, says they're always watchin' her and tellin' her what to do and stuff."

Ronni nodded. "Yeah, sounds like Bernadine. Always going off on my momma, telling her to mind her own business and to stop being so nosey. My momma can drive you crazy sometimes. She doesn't do anything all day except cook and watch TV and eat potato chips and complain. That's what Bernadine can't stand--momma's complaining all the time. I guess that's why she came out west."

"Hey, Ronni, do you guys have like somethin' to eat? Like cookies or potato chips or somethin'?" Suddenly, from a place deep within my stomach came a roaring desire for junk food.

"Sure," said Ronni, standing up. "I think we've got some chips. I'll get 'em." She left the room, at almost the same instant that the sliding glass door opened and Ritchie Lane and Morning Star stepped in.

"Hey, hey my man. It's time to jam." Ritchie walked over to the amps, fiddled with a couple of knobs and picked up an electric guitar. He ran his thumb across the strings, turned his head, listening with his mouth open, and then tuned it. He repeated this several times then played the opening bars to some song, and shook his head at me. "That's it, that's it. Now we gonna groove."

Ronni reappeared with a large bag of barbeque-flavored potato chips.

"Umm, girl, that's just what I want. Give them chips here," said Morning Star, reaching out.

"No way, Bernadine. They're for Del."

"Well, get a bowl then. Your boyfriend and I gots the munchies real bad. And stop callin' me by that nowhere name. I done told you before that's dead. That name don't apply no more. All that's dead and gone."

"But Bernadine, I can't call you Morning Star 'cause I grew up with my big sister named Bernadine, Bernadine." Smiling, Ronni skipped out of the room just in time to miss a cushion hurled at her head.

"You think you funny but you ain't, little girl," called out Morning

Star. She turned to me, glassy eyes moist, and spoke in a mock whisper, "Your girlfriend crazy. Sometimes I think she a square in black clothin'."

I beamed at Morning Star. I felt happy, content, relaxed, hungry. I smiled to myself and kept re-running in my head those weird and special words Morning Star had just used. Your boyfriend. Your girlfriend. If it had been in the schoolyard back in the town or if Davy or another one of my friends or even family had said this, I would have struck out with either fists or denials; probably both. But in this room rich with the deep warm grain of wood, here with lovely Ronni and beautiful Morning Star and Ritchie Lane and his magical music, on the plush, giving sensuousness of the pillowed floor, it was alright. Everything was alright.

Ronni set a bowl down on the floor and emptied the potato chips into it. I scooped out a large handful and consumed them ravenously.

"Hey, music man," Morning Star said to Ritchie, "stop fondlin' with that thang and throw down some jams."

For an answer, Ritchie pointed the head of his guitar at Morning Star and fired short, staccato electric riffs at her. Then he closed his eyes, spread his feet apart, moved his hands and fingers and the roof seemed to explode into the sky with a tremendous burst of sound, sound resonating within and pulling at a buried, hidden place in my chest that I didn't even know existed, sound lifting me up into the air, coruscating round my head in a sparkling shower of tiny stars. Ritchie Lane was transformed, his entire body a continuing flow of movement, arms and legs, torso and neck organic and alive. Eyes closed, lips slightly parted, head shaking back and forth, he appeared as if he were in a trance. I glanced over to Morning Star, who was leaning back on her extended arms, head uplifted and bobbing, eyes shut, a small Mona Lisa smile on her glowing face. Ronni sat next to me, head moving to the rhythms coming from Ritchie's guitar.

"*Walkin' by Myself*," called out Ritchie, launching right into the next song without a break. He called out other songs as he played them. *Train Kept A-Rollin', I Feel Fine, Paint it Black, Stone Free*. I had never heard a guitar make the sounds that Ritchie Lane made, and I had never heard most of the songs he played before. Listening to all this now, I knew that I wanted to be a rock star.

When he finished, we hooted and cheered and clapped our hands wildly. Ritchie curtsied like a princess, righted himself and made a low bow, one arm sweeping out in front of him. We all laughed and Ritchie put an LP on the record player, and sat down next to Morning Star. She bent towards him, opened her mouth, and he placed his opened mouth on hers. I could see their tongues pushing out against the insides of their cheeks. I guess I was staring at them, because Ronni punched me on the arm and gave me a certain look. The two finished with a wet smack.

Turning to me Ritchie asked, "Didya like that? The tunes, I mean!"

"Yeah, it was great. I wanna learn guitar. Will you teach me?"

"Sure, man. Anytime. Dig on this song by *Cream*," said Ritchie, tossing his head towards the record player. "Far out, ain't it? I dig the heavy bass line. Groove on the words, man."

I looked at the record player as if that would help me to listen better. Shaking my head I said, "I can't make it out."

"*You thought the leaden winter,*" sang Morning Star, "*Would bring you down forever/But you rode upon a steamer/To the violence of the sun'.*"

"And the chorus blows my mind, man. It goes like this: *'Tiny purple fishes go laughing through your fingers/and you want to take her with you/to the hard land of the winter'.*" Tripy, ain't it? I dig the guitar. That's where it's at, baby."

I nodded, foot tapping out the beat. "It's really neat," I said.

Ritchie reached behind him, and brought forth a carved wooden box inlaid with mother-of-pearl. Lifting the lid, he took out a folded square of paper, and raised his eyes to Morning Star. "Wanna take a trip, Star?"

"Mmm hmm. Sure do," smiled Morning Star. She opened her mouth, stuck her tongue out and Ritchie placed a flat thing that looked like a stamp on it, which Morning Star swallowed. Ritchie also ate one of these things.

"Ronni, Del--wanna do some?"

I opened my mouth to speak, but Ronni was quicker. "It's alright, Ritchie. We'll pass this time."

Ritchie nodded, said "Right on," and then stretched out flat on the floor. Ronni pulled my hand.

"C'mon," she said. "Let's go outside." We rose and went into the back yard.

"Why didn't you want to eat one of those stamp things?" I asked. "I was gonna take one of 'em. It's just like holy communion in church."

"You mean you were going to drop some?"

"No, I was going to eat it. What was it anyways?"

Ronni looked into my eyes. "You really don't know?"

I shook my head.

"That's acid."

"What's that?"

"Oh, come on, Del. You don't know what acid is? LSD?"

"Oh, yeah. I think I heard something about that on the news or somethin'. It's like a drug, right?"

"Right. It makes you see things. Colors and breathing walls and moving things. Stuff like that."

"Wow. Have you tried it?"

"No. Morning Star told me what it's like. I don't like stuff like that. Ritchie says it expands your mind and makes you feel things differently, but I don't know. There were some people back home who dropped it and they had real bad trips."

"What do you mean?"

"They saw giant spiders and weird monsters and one thought that the floor was lava and he kept screaming that his feet were getting all burned up. Some people go crazy because of it."

"Sounds bad."

"Yeah. I'll stick with my books. I like to have both of my feet flat on the ground."

We were walking around the fragrant garden, vibrant with the hum of dragonflies and hummingbirds buzzing around our heads. The sun, smiling and golden, floated high above, spinning down a gentle warmth on us and the graceful, peaceful flowers. Ronni's face seemed to catch the gold in the air, and her skin and eyes were radiant. But I felt sweat prickling the pits of my arms, and the palms of my hands grew wet and cold as my mouth dried. I coughed.

"Hey, Ronni?"

"Yeah?"

I coughed again. Coughing on a brilliant summer's day when I had no cold. "You gotta boyfriend back home? I mean, back in Detroit?"

"I guess I had one, but not anymore. He's stupid and I don't talk to him anymore. What about you, Del?"

"No. I don't have a boyfriend either."

"Ha ha. Very funny. Have you got a girlfriend or not?"

"Nope. Never had one. Most girls I know are stupid. All silly actin' and goofy and they don't like guys like me."

"What do you mean?" asked Ronni, looking into my face.

"I mean, I'm not on the football team or any team, and I don't have a job or a car and I got goofy hair-- "

"Wonderful hair."

"Yeah, well whatever--and I'm kinda thin."

"But I like you." Ronni was still looking into my face, so I looked at the ground.

"Yeah, that's great. I mean, I really like you, too."

"Great."

I let out a breath and smiled. "Yeah, great." Then a new wave of sweat broke out under my arms, but I didn't cough this time. "Great. And I like your sister, Morning--I mean Bernadine or whatever--I mean like back there in the house--" I turned awkwardly to point to the house--"she said to me, she said, 'your girlfriend,' about you and 'your boyfriend' and she was talkin' about me."

Ronni looked at me with smiles in her eyes.

I shrugged and scratched my nose. "So, like are you my girlfriend now?" I scratched my nose again.

"If you want me to."

"Wow. I mean, yeah sure. I just never had one before and all."

"Well now you do," said Ronni, "and I guess I've got a boyfriend, huh?"

"Yeah," I grinned, "Guess so."

"Great."

"Great."

After that I didn't know what to say or do and Ronni didn't say or do anything either, so we walked around the garden some more and talked. Once she touched my hand, and my whole body tingled and it felt good. Shadows began spreading out like purple fingers, and the sun turned deep yellow. It was time to go home. I went inside to say goodbye to Ritchie and Morning Star, but I don't think they heard me or even recognized me. Ritchie just sat on the floor, crossed legged, looking at, or rather watching something on the wall with great concentration. He was smiling and he kept saying things like, "*shhh*...listen... *shhhhh*...oh far out...far out, man," and Morning Star lay in a fetal position on the floor near an amp, tightly hugging a cushion to her body. She was laughing, but tears were streaming down her face. So, with a goodbye and a promise to come back soon to Ronni, I ran up the hill into the throbbing wildness of the late afternoon bush, alive with rabbits and squirrels and lizards and bluejays and I even saw a deer dimly in the chaparral, it's tanned hide mottled in blue and green, toothpick legs vanishing into the undergrowth, the whole animal itself fading into and out of vision like some dream creature as it pranced in between the luxuriant shafts of amber sunlight slanting down through the trees and bush, and the verdant pools of shadow where the sun could not reach.

With a head full of music and Ronni, images of the new born puppies and the gentle surrounding wonder of the land, I skipped and hopped and ran most of the way home, nearly forgetting--but not quite because of the dark clouds hanging on the fringes of my mind-- the night's sullen tragedy in the kitchen of the Ambassador Hotel. Maybe it had all been just a terrible dream. Maybe the thing that had happened had actually never happened. After all it was still the summer, and the days would never end. And if the day never ended, the night would never come.

9

But day became night became days into nights. Somehow the machinery of the world continued to grind the week following RFK's death. My dad drove off to work in the morning, returned late in the evening, had his whiskey or gin, bitched about something and fell asleep in the big chair while watching the news. As always. Kathy--when she was home--moped around the house in quiet sullenness or talked for hours in a hysterical, animated voice to various friends on the telephone. As usual. The Monster was content in her egotistical miniature universe, occasionally announcing her significance by a tantrum or by punching one of her older siblings. As ever. And the rusted iron teeth fitted into the cog which moved the rod that turned a wheel and the thing spun, not forward, but round and round. As forever.

My mom was different, though. She didn't speak much to anybody and for at least a week her eyes were bloated and ringed in red. When my dad was at work, the house was quiet and still. The Monster and I stayed outside for long periods to keep out of my mom's way, because if you spoke too loud around her or knocked something on the floor or if the Monster started a fight with me, she'd snap at us in a voice we'd never heard her use before. It wasn't just a mom-telling-the-kids-to-shut-up-or-else voice, but a voice edged and strained, like she was going to explode any minute. She seemed to be happiest while alone with her books which she submerged herself into as never before--and we kids gave her a wide berth.

I guess I wasn't much better. For a couple of days after that night, it seemed that every little thing got on my nerves. Duke barking. The hum of the refrigerator. The Monster asking me dumb questions. My dad's incessant voice, my mom's weird cooking. Late at night, when only crickets and bats and the groaning wood of the house were alive, I'd cry. Not very long, but so intense and coming from within such a deep place inside me that I'd quickly become exhausted and drop heavily into dreamless sleep.

Then came the magazines. *Life, Look, Newsweek*, all with the Story of the Moment on its front pages. But I read every issue from cover to cover, suddenly hungry for all the details of the man and his destroyer. I stared at the pictures of Bobby in final victory at the podium, smiling to his supporters, and at him on the kitchen floor, looking small and lost and ghostly in black-and-white, a stricken-looking Asian boy supporting his bleeding head.

One day while my mom was in the town shopping and I, bored and restless, was snooping around my parent's bedroom, I found a stack of old magazines on the floor in the corner of their closet. These were special issues which dealt with another Story of the Moment. Of a death in November. Of pictures--this time in vivid, shocking color-- featuring the other brother, him riding in a car, first waving then milliseconds later hands reaching up to his throat, his head exploding into a fine red mist. Of the screwed up, pained faces of people receiving the news, of the assassin's black-and-white TV death, of the long procession and the riderless horse with boots set reversed in the stirrups, and of a last, frail salute to the flag-draped coffin by a little boy in shorts.

In the closet I found other magazine back issues as well, many of which I carried to my room where I lay on the floor, flipping through the pages, learning about the decade and realizing for the first time that while I had been in school, playing dodge ball or war or tag, or watching TV or hiking in the hills, an age was happening. There were a lot of pictures of almond-eyed, thin girls in short skirts, gray politicians and chubby businessmen, slick ads for shiny new cars and refrigerators and underwear, but there were other pictures too, pictures that dominated each issue as the decade progressed and made the other images appear trivial. I read about riots in Los Angeles and Detroit, the killing of an intellectual in Harlem, marches in the south, violence on the streets of Paris and Berlin, and of a hard and bitter war in the jungles of Vietnam, which seemed to have culminated in a big battle at the beginning of this year, called Tet.

But despite these things, the brilliant summer days lengthened. Each morning, silken beams of warmth pulled me from sleep, birds sang in the cloudless arching blue, the grass yellowed into sweetly smelling shafts which waved and whispered in the hot summer's breezes. And there were the puppies. The Monster and I kept careful watch over them and Taffy, making sure the new mother had fresh water and a full food dish. One afternoon we sat on the ground near the doghouse, watching the puppies that were already beginning to move freely about.

"Lookit the black one there, Mary Ellen. See how he's pushin' the others around and always gettin' milk? He thinks he's the boss."

"That's my dog," said Mary Ellen, "I picked 'im out and mom said I can have 'im if I want so he's mine."

"Big deal. I don't want 'im even. I already picked mine and I got a name, too."

"Which one?"

"Not tellin'. It's a secret."

"Hey, tell me, that's not fair. If you don't tell me, I won't tell you mine."

I laughed. "Calm down, Mary Ellen. I was only joshin' you. It's that one on the end over there. He's white with black spots and has a puffy face. I'm namin' 'im Cochise, after an Indian chief."

"My dog's prettier."

"Whatcha gonna name 'im?" I said, refusing to take the bait.

"Frank," said Mary Ellen proudly.

"Frank? What a stupid name."

"Is not! Your dog's gotta stupid name!"

"Frank's not even a dog-name, it's a people-name. If you name 'im Frank all the other dogs'll laugh at him and the cats, too."

"Shuddup!" said Mary Ellen, her face turning scarlet. "It's not a stupid name. It's a nice name and if the other dogs make fun, he'll bite 'em and then they'll shut up."

"Suit yourself. He's not my dog."

There was the sound of a motor and Mary Ellen and I looked over our shoulders at the hill leading up to the driveway.

"Hey," said Mary Ellen, "daddy's home!"

"Yeah," I said looking into the truck's cab. "And he's got someone with 'im."

The pickup parked and my dad and another man got out, slamming their doors shut with a loud *doompf*!

"It's Eddie McGhee," said Mary Ellen.

The two men started walking over to where we sat, Eddie looking small up against my dad's bulk. Eddie always dressed exactly the same: lace-up work boots, light blue shirt with two pockets over the breast, a gray cap and baggy khaki pants with no belt so that when he bent over you saw half of his butt, white and hairy against the dirty tanned skin of his back.

"Hey, kids," said Eddie. He looked and sounded funny when he talked because he was missing several teeth and had a cleft lip.

"Hi, Mr. McGhee."

"How's old Taffy girl and the pups comin' along?" said my dad, leaning over and peering into the doghouse.

"Fine, dad," I said.

Mary Ellen stood up and pointed. "That one there's my dog, daddy. The black one. His name's Frank."

"Frank? Well, that's a hell of a fine name ya got there, Mary Ellen."

Mary Ellen turned to me and stuck her tongue out. "And that's Del's, dog, named ca-ca."

"Cochise."

"That's a dumb name. You got a dog picked out, daddy?"

"Naw. I don't need one. I got my hands full with you kids."

"We gonna keep 'em all, dad?" I asked.

"Hell no. We can't have no eight dogs runnin' round the joint tearin' hell out of things."

"What're we gonna do with 'em then?"

"Hell if I know. Give 'em away. You want one, Eddie?"

Eddie stroked his chin. "Don't rightly know, Johnny. I tink so. I could use a hound dog round de house, scare off de tramps and such. But I wouldna take one now. Critters is too damn small."

"Well, that's one down. You got some friends who'd take 'em, Del?"

I thought for a moment. "Yeah, maybe. Maybe Davy would if his mom lets 'im. And maybe too Ritchie Lane, the rock star guy over the hill."

"You ask 'em, then. I don't want these dogs around here once they're grown. C'mon, Eddie. Let's go get us somethin'."

"OK, Johnny. Been waitin' for you ta say dat."

My dad looked down at me. "You wanna come see, Del? We're tastin' a new batch of *Panther's Pee*."

"Sure," I said, springing to my feet. I was always eager to participate in little projects with my dad. He was so old and tired from work all the time that he never had time to play with me like the kids' dads on TV, so I took any chance I could to do something together with him.

We walked into the very back of the pole barn, dark and cool and smelling of grease and diesel fuel, rusted iron and wood shavings. "Switch on the light there, Del," said my dad. I ran my hand along the corrugated steel wall until my fingers felt the switch, which I flicked upwards. There was a click, a noticeable delay of a second, and the overhead florescent light flickered on. My dad and Eddie were standing next to a large copper kiln, with copper tubes twisting out of it like bronzed worms. A big glass gallon jar sat on the ground, a copper tube running into it. It was filled with a clear white liquid and on the homemade label pasted onto it, written in my dad's thin, shaky scrawl, were the words *Panther's Pee*. My dad turned a knob, reached down and picked up the jar, and then put a hand into one of his pants pockets and pulled out his lighter.

"C'mere, Del. Lookey here." My dad tipped the jar and poured the liquid into a large spoon that Eddie was holding. Then he handed me the jar, struck his lighter and put the flame onto the liquid in the spoon.

"See that?"

"No," I said. "I don't see anythin'."

"Git up closely, son," said Eddie. "Don't look at de spoon, look just a cunt hair up from it. Squintin' helps."

Squinting, I looked where Eddie had told me to, and then said, "Oh yeah," upon seeing the tiny blue tip of flame dancing above the spoon as the liquid disappeared.

"That's *Panther's Pee* for ya, boy," grinned my dad. "Grappa. 140 proof. Old Manuel, that Portagee farmer out on Edna Road done shown me how to brew it right." My dad took a shot-and-a-half glass off a nearby wooden crate, poured it full and drank it in one gulp. "Wow! Sonofabitch. Take a swig of that, Eddie, " he grinned, handing the glass to Eddie McGhee. Then his grin vanished as he turned his hard blue eyes on me. "But don't you tell nobody 'bout this, Del. It's liable to get around to the Feds and then they'd come, case the joint and then bust my ass. So keep quiet, you hear?"

"Yeah, OK."

My dad was still looking at me, staring at something on my face. He frowned, then said, "C'mere, over here under the light. Put your chin up, boy. Well, I'll be god damned. Eddie, lookey here."

Eddie stuck his gristly face into mine. "Hot damn," he said. "Your boy's gonna be a man 'fore ya know it, Johnny." His breath smelled like a mixture of bad red wine and the rotting bits of meat you sometimes find stuck between your back molars.

I rubbed my cheeks and chin. "What is it, dad? What's wrong with me?"

"Hell, ain't nothin' wrong, Del. When d'ya get them hairs on your chin? They been there for long?"

Surprised, I stroked my chin, for the first time feeling several stiff, wiry things sticking out of it. "Gosh," I said, "I don't know where they came from."

The two men laughed and looked down at me. My dad threw back another shot of *Panther's Pee*. "Couple more years on ya and you'll be a goddamned man, drivin' a rig and headin' off to the salt mines every mornin' just like your old man."

Eddie was smiling at me. "You gonna be de lady killer just like your pappy, eh Del?" His eyes glistened in the florescent light, two small glassy marbles shining out at me.

"Guess so," I shrugged, still rubbing my chin.

"Heh. Hear dat Johnny boy? 'I guess so,' he say. Hee hee."

"Yeah, he'll be raisin' hell with the girls in no time at all, alright."

"I wanna go see myself," I said. Then I spun around and ran back to the house, not stopping until I reached the bathroom. After locking the door, I stuck my face up close to the mirror and raised my chin. There they were--five dark brown sprouts. Turning my head to one side I scanned my skin for more signs, but found nothing. Still, what there was was impressive. I couldn't wait to tell Davy. He'd have a fit. Then I'd have to show Ronni. That'd make her love me even more.

I came out of the bathroom and headed down the hall to the living room, searching for my mom. I had expected to find her on the sofa, reading, but she wasn't there nor was she in my parent's bedroom. Walking through the empty kitchen, I went into the back yard, where I found her sitting on a white wicker chair, her legs stretched out on the seat of another chair. Her head was resting on the backrest, face up in the sun, her eyes closed and her arms folded across the book on her lap. I stepped up to her.

"Hey, mom, guess what."

"Yes?" she said, not opening her eyes.

"You gotta look at me first."

My mom took her face out of the sun, turned towards where the sound of my voice was coming, and opened her eyes.

"What it is, Del?"

"You gotta guess. You gotta look at me real good around the face area and then guess what's different, OK?"

I smiled as her eyes scanned my face. "See somethin'?" I said.

"No. What is it, a scar or a glass eyeball?"

"Naw," I laughed. "Lookit here, right on my chin." I jutted it out for her to see.

"Well, well. Now, that is impressive, young man. How long have you been growing it? It looks pretty long to me."

"Really? Wow. Gosh, I don't know when it started. Daddy saw it first."

"Is your father home so early?"

"Yup. He just drove up a while ago with Eddie McGhee."

"Eddie's here too? Well, I certainly hope he doesn't stay long. I can't stand that ignorant man. What are they doing?"

I looked at the ground. "Oh, I don't know. Messin' round in the pole barn."

"*Panther's Pee*," said my mom with a tinge of disgust in her voice. "All those two do together is get drunk."

"Eddie's gonna take one of the puppies he said. Daddy said he doesn't want to have a whole bunch of dogs runnin' around." I spoke rapidly, eager to avoid a discussion about Eddie and drinking and my dad. This was the most relaxed I had seen my mom in several days and I didn't want her mood to sour. "And Mary Ellen's picked a puppy already, an all-black one, and I got the one that's black and white and I named 'im Cochise."

My mother had leaned back and put her head into the sun again, and the warm syrup of its rays dripped onto her face. "Hmm," she said. "Cochise. Apache Indian chief, if I recall correctly."

"Yup. I think it's a far out name."

" Say 'yes.' 'Far out?' Where'd you pick up that?"

"Over at Ritchie Lane's."

My mom kept her eyes unopened. "Ritchie Lane. He's the young man who bought George Cobb's farm, isn't he?

"Yup".

"Yes.' I didn't know you go over there. What do you do with him?"

"Nothin' much. Sit around and stuff. He's got a real-life tepee. Sometimes he plays his guitar. I'm gonna ask him and Ronni if they wanna have a puppy 'cause we got to get rid of 'em."

"Who's Ronni?"

"Just this girl whose sister is Ritchie Lane's girlfriend."

"What's she look like?"

"Who, the sister?"

"No, this Ronni."

"I don't know. Black curly hair, kinda skinny, eyes shaped like the eyes on those statues in that big book on Egypt you've got. I guess she's kinda cute, maybe."

"What color is she?"

I looked at my mom's face glowing in the honeyed light, and tried to read something there before I answered. It was like the Sphinx's. "She's black," I said.

I could see my mom's body stiffen and her face turn from sun toasted brown to just a shade darker. Like a stone, her head dropped out of the sun again and the eyes cut over to me, shiny and hard. "I see."

I knew I had just said something I shouldn't have.

"How black?"

"Whaddayya mean?"

"What I mean is she dark brown, milk chocolate, blue-black, caramel, cream, yellowish or very light?"

"I don't know," I said, unable to contain a slight resentfulness in my voice. "Who cares?" I shifted my feet.

My mom looked at me squarely, all the humor gone out of her face now. "Plenty of people care, Del, you know that. Don't play the innocent little boy with me."

I shoved my hands into my pants' pockets and tightened my shoulders. "I'm not playin' anythin'."

"You're not a child anymore. You're an intelligent young man able to see what the world is like. You'll have to start thinking of your future sometime soon and this Connie girl-- "

"Ronni."

"-- Ronni, will make problems and complications for you that you cannot now foresee."

"What are you takin' about? We're just friends is all."

"Watch your tone, Del. Don't you raise your voice with me."

"I'm not raisin' my voice. I'm just sayin' that Ronni's just a friend like Davy's a friend. That's all."

"No girl is 'just a friend' to a boy. How old is she?"

"I don't know. My age, I guess, maybe a year older. What does it matter?"

"Girls mature quicker than boys, they grow up faster and they know what they want and how to attract a boy's attention. Especially fast black girls. Don't be seduced by their jazzy talk."

"What?"

"Don't look at me with those goggle eyes. You know exactly what

I'm talking about."

"Mom, Ronni speaks better English than dad, than me even. I can't believe you're tellin' me this stuff."

"Believe it. It's for your own good. This is reality."

"But you sound like some kind of racist or somethin'," I said, feeling my head buzzing with the heat of anger and incredulity. My mom's eyes transformed into obsidian and she swung her feet off the chair and planted them solidly on the red brick underneath. "I am *not* a racist," she said with clenched jaws, "as you very well know. I simply want you to avoid certain unpleasantries."

"But she's just a friend."

"She's black and that is, unfortunately, all that counts in our society. She's not like Davy and under no circumstances will you invite her over here. Your father would have a fit."

"But she's a nice person."

"I'm quite sure she is but your father doesn't care. *I'm* the one who has to deal with his rages, not you. I'm the one in the middle. I've got my hands full between him and Kathleen and I don't want you complicating things more." Glowing hot, my mom's eyes bored into me and looked terrible in her now darkening face.

"Great," I spit out, "I won't ask her over. I won't ask any of my friends over ever again and that'll be just great!" Then I turned around and ran off to the house, slamming the door as I entered.

Stomping into the kitchen, I came upon Kathy leaning against the counter near the open window. She held a half-eaten stalk of celery in one hand and wore a thin smile on her face. "Boy, what was that all about?"

"Nothin'," I said, stopping. "Mom's just being a creepy jerk."

"She's been freakin' out the last couple of weeks. I'm glad to see someone else gettin' screamed at for once. Usually I take all the heat." With a crisp snap, Kathy bit off a piece of celery. The smile was just visible in her eyes and at the corners of her mouth.

"Yeah, well, if mom's in a bad mood she shouldn't take it out on us kids."

Kathy stepped closer to me, smiling grimly. "Now maybe you understand what I go through all the time. Every time I open my mouth or try to do somethin' with my friends, mom and dad always start trippin'. Then I get called the troublemaker. It's no fun around here. Everybody's trippin'."

"Yeah," I nodded, "you can't win."

"And it's gonna be hell here on Saturday. God, if I can't invite my friends, I swear I'll lock myself up in my room and blast the radio to block out the noise."

"What do you mean? What's goin' on Saturday?"

"You know, dummy."

"I do?"

"Daddy's b-day. There's gonna be a big party and everyone's goin' to come and I want to invite my friends 'cause it's not fair to have to hang out with borin' old people all the time."

"Gosh, I clean forgot about it. I wanna invite Davy. They gotta let Davy come. I'll ask mom."

"Well, don't do it now or she'll say no."

"No duh. I'll give her a couple hours to cool down."

Kathy popped the last of the celery into her mouth, and ground it between her teeth. "She's got to say yes to us or it'll be totally unfair. If I can't invite my friends, then I'm gonna run away for sure."

"Yeah," I said, feeling closer to Kathy then I had in months. "Me, too."

10

Spinning on her heel, Kathy turned from me and headed out into the hall. Suddenly realizing where she was going, I dashed after her and caught her just as her hand lifted the receiver.

"Wait! Kathy--can I make a quick call to Davy before you start talkin' on the phone for the rest of the day?"

Kathy looked at me with one hand on her hip, and sighed with annoyance. "How long will you be?"

"Just a sec. I wanna invite Davy to daddy's b-day. I bet it's gonna be a barbeque like last year and I don't wanna be stuck with all those dumb grown-ups."

Kathy stared at me. Smiling, I approached and picked up the receiver.

"Exactly one second. Promise?"

"Promise," I said, dialing. The phone rang for a long time and I was just about to hang up when it clicked.

"Hello?" said a thick, muffled voice.

"Um, Mrs. Peterson?"

"Yes. Who's speaking please?"

"Oh, hi. It's Del, Davy's friend. Can I speak to 'im?" Then I remembered who I was talking to. "Um, please?"

Davy's mom let out a heavy sigh before answering. "Well, I don't know if Davy wants to speak to anyone just now. I'll...I'll just see. Please hold on, Del, I'll..." and her voice trailed off weirdly. I glanced at

Kathy, who was glaring at me, arms folded across her chest. "His mom's gettin' 'im," I smiled weakly.

"One second." She held up a finger to help make the point.

Davy's mom was gone a long time, so I kept my eyes on my feet and didn't look up in Kathy's direction again, although I was aware of her pacing back and forth. Then, coming from inside the receiver, I heard softly padding footsteps followed by the thumping and banging sounds of someone fumbling with the phone. Mrs. Peterson said, "Damn it!" in a distant voice but then suddenly louder and nearer came, "Hello, Del? I'm sorry about that. It seems that Davy doesn't, can't come to the phone right now. He doesn't feel well."

"Oh. Jeepers, is he sick or somethin'?"

There was another sigh, and another pause, and finally Mrs. Peterson's choked, whispered voice. "No, no. Davy's OK. He's alright, it's just that...oh, we've just got some bad news here. Terrible. Davy's brother...we've just been informed that Davy's older brother has been killed in Vietnam."

"Oh, gosh, Mrs. Peterson. I'm so sorry."

"Yes."

"Gosh," I stammered, "that's really rotten."

"Yes, yes." Her voice sounded small and far away. "Now if you'll excuse me, Del, I think I'll go. I really don't..." her voice failed again.

"Oh, yeah sure. Gosh, I'm real sorry Mrs. Peterson. Tell Davy, please, tell him he can call me if he wants to talk or somethin'."

"Yes. Fine. Thank you for calling, Del. Goodbye."

"Goodbye." Slowly, I hung the receiver back on its hook and stood there staring at it. My shoulder was shoved and Kathy said, "Move."

"Cut it out," I snapped.

"That was way more than a second."

"Shuddup."

"Shuddup yourself," snarled Kathy. "That's the last time you go first on the phone again you little ass."

"For you information Miss Butt Wipe, I was talkin' to Davy's mom."

"So?"

"So Davy's big brother just got killed in Vietnam."

With grim satisfaction, I watched the surprise register on Kathy's face and all the petty anger draining out of it. "Oh," she said. "Bummer."

"Yeah," and I turned and walked off to my room.

I laid flat on my stomach on my bed in my room, my small airplanes floating helplessly above me, silent dusty shelves towering up towards the ceiling, the maniac plastic orangeness of the bean bag shapelessly cold and dead, wrinkled and motionless on the floor beneath my chin. I had met Davy's brother only once. He was a grown-up and I never had much to do with him though I knew how much Davy looked up to him. I remembered that he had short hair and small eyes, a thick Marine neck and a big chest, and he didn't smile too much; but maybe he had nothing to smile about. And there was a picture of him I'd seen a couple of times, placed on a chest of drawers in the living room. He was boxed in by a silver frame, in his Marine uniform, white peaked hat, tight fitting dark blue tunic with brass buttons, and he was still not smiling. But then I guess soldiers never smile.

And that was all I knew about Davy's big brother except that he was on his second tour of duty in Vietnam, stationed...I tried to recall the name, but couldn't. Getting up from the bed, I went to my bookcase and pulled out an atlas, flipped to South East Asia and gazed at the map of the war land, the funny sounding names of places I sometimes heard on TV or saw in the news magazines. Mekong Delta. Hue and Da Nang. The Highlands. Phnom Penh. War places filled with thousands and thousands of Gone People. They marched into the green bellies of giant airplanes over here and flew away across the sea-- several seas--and you saw them briefly on the news and then you didn't see them again, forever; they never seemed to come home in the airplanes that took them away. But other planes brought them back in flag-draped boxes.

I snapped the book shut and slipped it back into its place on the shelf, then sank down on the floor and pulled out my box of little men. It seemed like years since I had last played with them. Looking at their small plastic forms piled into a great heap of sprawling arms, spread legs, tiny hands clutching tiny spears and bows and rifles and swords, heads bonneted with helmets and feathers, soft caps and cowboy hats, they all looked so silly to me, bent into action positions--running, crawling, kneeling, falling--and yet going nowhere. Between thumb and forefinger, I pinched one out of the khaki, green, blue pile and twirled him slowly before my eyes. The plastic felt dead in my hand. No warmth. No softness. No life. I released my hold and he tumbled stiffly into the box with his comrades. Then I slid the box under my desk. I didn't want to play them anymore.

Sitting on the floor with my legs crumbled up beneath my body, my back resting against my bed, my mind flickered back to the conversation in the yard with my mom. That was unbelievable. A betrayal of me, of herself, of RFK. My hand balled up and struck the wooden floor. Oh, my stupid dad. Why did he have to be that way? Hadn't he learned anything after surviving the Depression and two world wars, any empathy or understanding for others, inside his family or not? Was RFK's and MLK's message too opaque to be understood? It made me angry how he dominated life in our home, how he set the rhythm and the mood. My dad: a trembling mass of muscle, tissue and nerve, full of prejudices and fears and insecurities--living around him was like playing hop-scotch in a minefield. Sooner or later your foot would land where it shouldn't have, and *ka-boom!* the earth erupted.

It didn't make any sense. Why couldn't Ronni come over, this skinny, little preteen with almond shaped eyes and sunlight in her smile? She was either a good person or not. A friend to have fun with or someone to forget. That was all. What was so threatening about that?

Our family was screwed up, I decided. The TV told you exactly how it should be: Father wore a white shirt and a thin black tie and drove away at seven-thirty in the morning after eating fried eggs and toast and a cup of good coffee, and Mother put on her apron and smiled and hummed to herself while scrubbing the toilet bowl and cooking the evening meal and she never got dirty herself and she never even sweated and her skin was waxy with light, and the Children--Tad, Mary and June--diligently did their homework, played with their gleaming new toys and waited for Father to return from a good, hard day at the office so they could all sit down at the dinner table and

O'Brien Browne

watch Father carve the roast beef while Mother, still smiling, served the carrots and peas and glasses of milk, and later everyone gathered around the warmly glowing TV and were happy. But our family couldn't get it right. There was something wrong with us. We were freaks.

I stood up, sucking in air from my opened mouth. My room, which with each passing day appeared smaller and more confining and stale to me, felt hot and sticky, so I went outside. Mary Ellen was still at the doghouse, sitting on the ground. Frank, her puppy, was in her lap, asleep, while the other puppies roamed around.

I sat down next to Mary Ellen and scratched Frank on the head. He shifted a paw, but did not open his eyes.

"Watch out," said Mary Ellen. "Don't wake him up."

"I won't. Where's Cochise?"

"Over there. He's fightin'."

Just beyond the doghouse, I saw Cochise, a long stick in his mouth. He was trying to carry it away but another puppy, with white paws and a white tail, had one end of it in his mouth and was attempting to drag it in the opposite direction.

"They're funny," I laughed to Mary Ellen as two puppies bounded over to Cochise and crashed into him. The puppies were getting fat now, and their fur had become sleek and glossy, their faces puffy and their tails curled up like piglet tails. I laughed at how they tumbled about on their short little legs, their paws big and soft and awkward, looking like white-gloved clown's hands. They were so small and cute, goofy and full of bouncing, dancing life. Cochise ran past me, and I scooped him up with one hand and held him up to my face. His smiling mouth opened, revealing a soft pink tongue. Button nose and button eyes reminded me of Mary Ellen's stuffed animals. Setting the pup back on the ground, he scampered off and bit one of his siblings on the back, and together they rolled into a ball of fur and dust. Watching them made me feel better.

I leaned back on my elbows and gazed skyward. It was a bleached blue day, the sun high and hot and riding miles above in a flame of white.

"Boy is it hot out here," I said.

"Yup. Lookey here. I gotta burn."

I examined where Mary Ellen's short, fat finger pointed to a glowing red patch on her thigh.

"That's a burn alright. You oughta put some cream on it or the skin'll turn dead and fall off like a snake's."

"OK."

"C'mon," I said, standing up and slapping the dust from my hands and pants. "Let's get outta the sun. I'll make us up some lemonade and you can rub yourself down with cream."

Just then a loud burst of laughter came out of the pole barn and I turned to see my dad and Eddie McGhee emerging from its shadows. As they drew near to me and the Monster, I noticed that Eddie stumbled as he walked. Both men were grinning and my dad's face was red; Eddie's, on the contrary, was pale gray but his eyes, pink and glossy, blinked out from dark caves in his face. My dad stood in front of me with his legs spread apart and his hands plunged into his pockets.

"Hey, Del," he said.

"Hi, dad," I said a bit sullenly.

"How's the ole hound dogs doin?'"

"Fine, I guess."

Eddie stood next to my dad, smiling toothlessly and wavering on his thin bowed legs which appeared as firm and stable as rubber bands.

"Heh, heh," he laughed slurredly, "Dem old doggies is funnier'n hell boy, how dey tumble 'bout 'n such."

"And I'm hungrier'n' hell," said my dad and Eddie laughed again although I didn't see any joke. "Your mom's inside, ain't she?"

"Sure daddy," answered Mary Ellen. "Where else she'd be?"

"Heh-heh, she got ya dere, Johnny boy."

"I sure as hell hopes she's cooked up dinner already. That grappa makes a man hungry. She cookin'?"

"Don't know," I said, "Last I saw her she was in the back yard with a book."

"Readin'. Hell."

"Hell," echoed Eddie, then he burped loudly, which made Mary Ellen giggle. "Johnny, your wife be readin' too much n' her goddamn eyes gonna pop right oudda her head if she ain't carefi."

"That's what I tell her."

"Well, what's she say ta dat?"

"Nuthin'. She just picks up a book and starts readin' again."

"Heh, heh, heh," chuckled Eddie, and my dad even cracked one of his rare smiles himself.

"C'mon you drunken sonofabitch," said my dad, turning toward the house, "let's go 'n get us some eats." Watching my dad move toward the kitchen, I could see there was a slight zigzag in his stride.

"What's a-matter with Eddie, Del? He looks like a dead man," asked Mary Ellen.

"He ain't--isn't--dead, Mary Ellen. Just drunk. Let's go inside now."

We went into the kitchen, which my dad and Eddie had just passed through because the air was heavy with a sour, sweaty, dirty smell. I took a jar of sun cream off the top of the refrigerator, then stooped down, put my hands under Mary Ellen's arms and lifted her onto the table. Pulling a chair up, I sat down in front of her and squirted some cream into my hand, and rubbed it onto her leg.

"Ow."

"What's a-matter--burns?"

"Yeah, but a hot-cold burnin'."

"That's OK--it's suppose to do that. That means it's workin'. Stop kickin'."

"It's a creepy feelin'," said Mary Ellen, "and I don't like it."

At that moment, I heard an outburst of voices coming in through the open kitchen window. Mary Ellen started kicking again. "Ow, Del. You're rubbin' too hard."

"*Shhhh*," I hissed, straining to hear the voices, which sounded angry. "Here, take it Mary Ellen. You can put it on yourself." Handing her the cream, I rose and stood near the window. In the back yard I saw my mom, still sitting in the wicker chair with Eddie and my dad standing in front of her. Her arms were crossed.

"If you want something, go fix yourselves a sandwich," my mom was saying in a loud, stern voice.

"Well, hell honey," said my dad with a grin, "a sandwich ain't no kinda meal. We're hungry. How 'bout fixin' up some dinner?"

"I'm not making dinner now. It's too early."

"Well, ya gotta fix it sooner or later."

"I choose later. I want to finish what I'm reading first."

"Hell, that'll take all day."

"Don't be ridiculous."

"Me and Eddie's hungry and I'll bet the kids is, too."

"I'm damn near starved," said Eddie, meekly.

"Will you please let me get back to my book?" said my mom, ordering, not asking.

"Why the hell do you always gotta be readin' for?"

"Why are you always drunk?"

"Goddamn it," my dad's voice rose to a shout, "I ain't always drunk! A man's gotta have his fun sometimes."

"And a woman, too."

"Maybe a sandwich'd be OK, huh Johnny?" tossed in Eddie.

"What the hell's goin' on here? You're a wife for Christ sakes and you're suppose to be cookin' for the family."

"When I'm good and ready."

"'Tink some fruit would be just fine," said Eddie.

"Jesus H. Christ, you care more 'bout them damn books of your's than me 'n the kids."

"You know that's utter nonsense."

"You just sit 'round the house all day readin' 'bout some dead old English bastards and I'm out there tryin' like a sonofabitch to provide you and the kids with food and a roof over your heads and you can't even make me dinner," my dad's face was beet red and his eyes burned like blue jet flames, "and the next thing I know you gonna run off to night school when you got a house and growin' kids to be takin' care of."

"Can I get me a glass a-wadder?" asked Eddie in a mouse squeak.

My mom shot up from her chair and tucked her book firmly under her arm. Her face was set hard and solid like concrete and the veins stood out in chords in her neck. "Johnny, don't you dare tell me how to raise my children. Don't you dare talk to me about motherhood and responsibilities. I'm sick of your rages and your getting drunk with your ignorant friends and your trying to determine my life. Sick of it all, do you hear me?" My mom took a step towards my dad and he moved half a step backwards. "I'm fed up with all this crap I have to put up with day after day and if you don't watch it, I'll, I'll...God knows what I'll do." My mom stopped abruptly, her body leaning forward like she was leaning over a precipice, knuckles gleaming white on her fists, chin jutted out. Her eyes were fired coals, her feet were planted firmly on the brick patio floor and her chest rose and fell as hot air rushed in and out of her flared nostrils.

My dad stared at her hard for a moment, then turned his head and spat. "Christ," he said. "Jesus H. Christ. C'mon, Eddie. Let's go back to the pole barn." He turned away from my mom's gripping gaze, and with Eddie--head tucked down between his bony shoulders--weaving behind him, both were gone. My mom stood rigid, watching them go, then unfroze and slowly sank back down in the chair, put up her legs and opened her book. After a second though, she slammed it shut and started biting on a thumbnail. When I turned away from the window, she was still sitting in the same position, gnawing on her nail and staring out beyond the garden, on past the distant hills and, it seemed to me, out beyond the summer itself.

11

High summer, and each day unfolded long and hot, dry and windless, angry and glorious and brutal. Local ranchers said they hadn't seen such a heat wave for two decades and that all the ground water would be sucked dry and we'd have a drought come fall. The tall grass mummified into pale yellow sticks of brittleness, the arid earth became hard yet powdery and when you walked tan clouds of dust rose up out of the impressions your feet left behind you in the ground. The back yard's daisies withered under the sun's hammer and only in late afternoon when my mom sprinkled them with water from the garden hose, did they raise their heads again to the blistered sky. Duke and Taffy crept into the pole barn and lay panting in its shadows, and Smokey stayed under the big tree shading his water trough for hours on end, his huge head bowed down low to blow at the crusty earth as fat, greasy flies droned drunkenly around his eyes and hindquarters, scattering momentarily from the slow swish of his tail.

The pond had long since dried up. Now it was only an empty dent in the earth's desert surface, layered by a dry and stiff crust of moss, bleached pale green by the sun. At its bottom were pieces of wood, large stones and a plastic Spanish galleon and a W.W. II submarine I had lost during the rainy time in February. There was no trace of the frogs, and I wondered how they could have vanished so completely when there was no place for them to go.

The puppies were the only green of life. There were six, and no runts among them, all being healthy and energetic and alert. They seemed to prosper in the heat despite their fluffy coats, and spent all day tumbling over each other, chasing their own tails, yelping and sinking their emerging teeth into anything they could find. Cochise was, of course, my special pet and I played with him for hours at a time, dragging a piece of string behind me for him to chase, playing hide 'n seek, rolling him over onto his back and scratching his belly as he tried to bite my hand. I would slip him tidbits from the kitchen table and feed them to him late at night. On several occasions, after my parents had gone off to bed, I crept outside, tucked Cochise under my arm and sneaked him into my bed, where he slept with me. I'd wake up early in the morning to his rough, moist tongue licking my face, and transport him outside before my parents got up.

After my mom and dad's big fight, things cooled down even as the heat increased. Maybe the sun drained them of energy or maybe my dad was just too tired after work or maybe my mom was too busy taking care of us kids and planning for my dad's birthday party on Saturday, but they didn't go after each other so much any more. My mom was almost in a good mood sometimes, like in the old days before the summer ever came, but sometimes she got real quiet and thoughtful and she'd sit on the sofa in the living room, not even watching TV or reading but only looking far away out the window and it seemed like she wouldn't blink for hours at a time. My dad was never that way. He was either total, kinetic energy, half-drunk and mellow or dead asleep. One or the other. When he got mad, he'd scream and bitch and cuss, red-faced, wild-eyed and out of control. Then, seconds later, it'd all be forgotten and he'd pour himself a drink, settle into his big chair in front of the TV and drift away to wherever it was he went to when not planning, working, fighting, building, sleeping or yelling.

One afternoon, I came into the kitchen and found my mom at the table, writing. I didn't hate her as much as I had after our shocking conversation about Ronni, so I sat down, leaned my elbows on the tabletop, set my chin into my upturned palms and said,

"Whatcha doin'?"

"Making a list."

127

"What kinda list?"

"For Saturday. It's going to be a big party."

"We gonna barbeque?"

"Yes. There'll be steaks and ribs and pork chops and Italian sausage."

"Wow."

"And I'll make some salads, as well--a big Caesar's and a pasta salad, too."

"What's a pasta?" I asked.

"Noodles, I mean."

"Oh. Why didn't you say so? You gonna make--?"

"Are you."

"Are you gonna make potato salad, too, and garlic bread?"

"Oh yes, of course. I forgot the bread," said my mom, writing.

"Who all's gonna come anyways?"

"My mom glanced down at her list."Let's see, there'll be Eddie McGhee and his wife Marge, Kay Lifton-Wright--"

"Better buy lots of booze."

"Don't be mean, Del. And Wanda, and a couple of local ranchers from down the hill, Doc Mathews the vet, Jake and Hal from the hardware store, and then Al Wainwright--"

"Oh no, and his creepy wild man sons?"

"Yes. What's the matter with Al's sons?"

"They're creeps. They're all big like grown ups and they already have hair on their faces and they get into fights down in the town and stuff."

"We'll they'll behave themselves here, I'm sure. They won't try any funny business with your father around." My mom put the pen to her lips. "And who else? Oh, yes, Kathy's boyfriend Ernie and a couple of her friends from school--if your father doesn't have any loud objections, that is."

"Jeepers. That's a lotta people."

"Not really. We've had more over before. This time we're trying to keep it a bit more manageable. And what about you, Del, would you like to invite Davy?"

"Gee, I don't know. I forgot to tell you that I tried callin' him a couple of days ago and his mom answered and she said that Davy can't talk 'cause his big brother got killed in Vietnam."

My mom's eyebrows arched. "What? Oh, that's terrible. When did this happen?"

"Dunno. Musta been in the last week or so. It's rotten, huh?"

My mom shook her head. "My god, what a stupid, stupid waste."

"Yeah. Why don't they end it? A lotta guys are gettin' killed over there and seems like every week it only gets worse and worse."

"That makes me furious." She shook her head again. "That poor young man. My god, what a time we're living in, what an awful, brutal time. I'm going to give Davy's mother a call right now."

"Tell her 'hi' from me to Davy and that he should come over Saturday if he's feelin' OK again. Maybe it'd like make him feel better and stuff."

My mom got up and went to the phone, and I left, not wanting to hear her conversation. It'd only be sad and I just wasn't up to listening to more tragedy; it seemed like each day in this summer brought new reports of violence somewhere on the planet, police violence, the violence of machines, gun violence, fists, knives, mass industrial plastic chemical violence. So I slipped away into my room, closing the door firmly behind me.

Once inside, I was instantly bored. I had no interest in my dust-covered toys, and so pulled up the mattress and took out the two magazines Davy had brought what now felt like years ago. I flipped through the well-worn glossy pages as I had done countless times before, only this time I didn't feel like doing it. My room was so small and cramped, the air so flat and motionless, and the heavy-lidded, smiling women in lace and garters, their curvy bodies bending into mysterious sublime contortions, did not hold the old interest for me. I wanted out. And I knew where out.

As I passed the pole barn on my way up the hill and along the trails through the chaparral, Cochise bounded out at me, barking happily, and I swept him up in my arms and carried him with me for companionship.

I found them in the music room, listening to *Cream*. Ritchie Lane and Morning Star where both smoking Mary Jane, the bluish smoke of which was so pleasing to me, carrying with it pleasant mellow feelings of Ritchie's home, filled with music and the warmth of dark grained wood, the tepee outside in the sun surrounded by grass and flowers and a dark shivering pattern of gently swaying tree branches and leaves etched in shadow on its surface. Ronni was in the kitchen, doing something at the counter. Her back was to me.

Holding my breath, I tip-toed up behind her as she worked, and held Cochise's muzzle against her ear. His tongue flicked out.

Ronni gave a yelp of surprise and jumped to one side. Then her eyes widened and her face brightened with her warm, beautiful smile. "Del! I never heard you come sneaking in. Where'd you get him?" she said, coming forward to pet the puppy. "He's so cute."

"His name's Cochise, a puppy from our dog."

"Can I have him?" Ronni took him from my arms and stroked her cheek across the top of his head.

"Well, ah... he's kinda my dog, Ronni. But we got four others and you can have one of 'em if you want."

"Really?"

"Sure. We gotta get rid of 'em anyways."

"Wow. I'd love to take one. I have to show him to Bernadine."

"Ronni," I said. "Lemmie ask you somethin'. Why come you never call Morning Star Morning Star?"

"Because that's not her real name."

"So what? If she wants a new name, who cares?"

Ronni, petting Cochise, leaned against the kitchen counter. "Because it's not right, Del. It's not right. Bernadine is her name and it's a nice name. It's the name she grew up with. It's historical, also, in our family. My momma's momma was called Bernadine, and a couple of our cousins are, too. Bernadine is a good name and it's real, not made up. Bernadine should keep what's been given to her like something special, like it was a treasure."

"Then why come she calls herself Morning Star?"

Ronni spoke only after thinking for a moment. "I think because she wants to forget about our family and Detroit and our dad and stuff. She thinks she can run away from herself, her roots, and sneak into some kind of newer, other person. And that ain't, I mean, it isn't right.

She shouldn't play like that. She can't just get away like that. It won't work. I'm never going to do that. Run off, I mean. Never ever."

"Well, maybe she's sick of stuff back home, like my big sister. Maybe nobody listens to her and so she figures, why hang around?"

"But running off," said Ronni, "is just running away."

"Huh?"

"I mean, that means you never have to deal with the situation. You can just split when you don't like what other people are saying or doing."

"Maybe so," I said, "I don't know. You should meet my big sister. She's always talkin' about runnin' away and stuff. She's like totally sick of my parents."

"Why?"

"Oh, you know. They get on your nerves. They can kinda be naggin' sometimes, and my dad gets kinda wild. He's always screamin' and yellin' 'bout somethin' and he don't --"

"Doesn't."

"--Yeah, doesn't --" I smiled, "let you say anythin'. Sometimes you just wish he'd shut up."

"Well, you and your sister should be glad you've got a daddy."

"Well, sometimes we wished we had another one. I think even my mom wishes that, too."

"Be glad with what you've got. My daddy ran off and it's been real hard on my momma. I'm never going to do my family like that. I'm going to raise my family good, get a job and have a nice house and a nice family and stay put. I'm not going to run away."

"You'll be just like Ozzie and Harriet on TV."

"Yeah," laughed Ronni. "TV perfect."

Just then Morning Star burst into the room, her tall, sleek body moving with an easy, sensual grace. "Where's the fuck my peanut butter sandwich, girl? Damn, I'm starvin'. Whatcha ya'll doin' back here anyway all quiet and shit? Gettin' down or what?"

"Shush, Bernadine, don't be nasty. Here it is." Ronni handed her big sister the sandwich. I couldn't help noticing the look on Ronni's face, an older, grown-up look of displeasure that mothers get when annoyed with a naughty child. Ronni often had that look; Morning

Star never.

"Hey you old hound dog," said Morning Star, rubbing her nose into Cochise's fuzzy face. "Dog, you just as sweet as your owner, ain'tcha?" Morning Star turned from the puppy and smiled at me, a smile that was every bit as warm and delightful as Ronni's but with something else in it, too, something dangerous and knowing and inviting and deliciously wicked. She had this way of eyeing me like she knew some deep secret of mine that I didn't even know about myself yet. She looked good in a short buckskin skirt that rode high up on her thighs, and a buckskin vest with feathers and strips of leather dangling from it. I swallowed hard, looking at the long elegant curves of her smooth legs, the roll of her hips and that wicked, wicked smile. She had a way of making me feel things I had never felt before in the world outside of my room. She almost made me feel grown up.

Ronni was not leaning against the counter anymore, but standing up straight, unsupported, arms crossed.

Morning Star looked up at her sister, eyes twinkling. "Don't you worry none, little girl, I ain't goin' after your sweet thang."

"Be quiet, Bernadine," said Ronni, as I blushed. I didn't really understand the full meaning within Morning Star's words, but they sounded good in a naughty way, and I liked hearing her say them.

Morning Star laughed and bit into her sandwich, not tearing with her teeth but pulling the soft, delicate bread with a pursing of her lips, with just a flash of tongue, pink and moist, snaking behind the smooth row of teeth. We followed her out of the kitchen and into the main room where Ritchie sat on a cushion, reading the back of an album. Morning Star sat down next to him and they kissed with open mouths, which caused my stomach to feel ticklish. Ronni and I found cushions and rested on them as Cochise squirmed out of Morning Star's arms and scampered to me, his claws clicking on the wooden floor.

"How many pups you say you got, man?" asked Ritchie Lane.

"Six. Four really, 'cause I took Cochise and my little sister has one. Actually there's only three if my dad's friend takes one of 'em."

"We oughta take one, huh Star?"

"Oooo yes. I'd like two. Can't have no dog all alone; that ain't fair. Gots to have at least two so's they can keep theyselves company."

"Yeah," said Ronni, "I've never had a dog before. Let's take a couple, Ritchie."

"Hope they're healthy, Del. Don't want no puppies with some weird-ass dog disease like rabies or distemper or hoof 'n mouth or some such shit, dig?"

"Yeah, Ritchie, they're healthy alright," I said, "Just look at Cochise." I held the dog up facing them, his little paws dangling and his tiny tongue protruding from his round face. "Nothin' will ever happen to him," I said.

"Fuck man," smiled Ritchie, "you can't say no to such a cute face like that."

Ronni took Cochise from my hands. "He's sooo cute. I hope the others are just as adorable."

"They are. Promise. If you don't like 'em, there's a full money back guarantee."

"Far out, baby. Just like at *Sear's*." Ritchie Lane rose up on his knees and hobbled over to the record player. He very carefully slipped the LP which he had been reading out of its jacket and held it between the palms of both of his hands. After examining it closely, he blew on it and placed it gently onto the player. He swung the stylus over and set it down onto the spinning vinyl.

"Grove on this. This stuff'll blow your mind," said Ritchie, adjusting a few knobs on the receiver.

"Who is it?"

Ritchie crawled to his girlfriend and say alongside her. "Hendrix. It's a far out tune called *Third Stone from the Sun*."

"Oh wow. We oughta drop, Ritchie," said Morning Star.

"Yeah. That'd be far out." Ritchie Lane slid down onto his side and reached out to the wooden mother-of-pearl box. "The *box*," he intoned earnestly. Flipping it open, he took out an envelope, snapped the lid shut and sat upright again. Morning Star turned her face toward Ritchie, closed her eyes and out unrolled the long, wet snake of her tongue. Ritchie took a thin square and placed it on her tongue, which Morning Star drew in and, with her back up against the sofa, eyes still closed, leaned her head back. In the background the music played, a slow rolling bass above the lion-purr of the guitar, a buzzing-humming sound, weirdly whispered voices and the hollow moan of wind blowing on a flat desert plane.

Ritchie Lane placed a stamp on his tongue and then leaned over and handed the envelope to me. "You do your own thing, man. There's one more tab in there. You guys can split if you want."

I took the enveloped and looked inside.

"No thanks," said Ronni.

"Oh, girl, get with it. Don't be so square."

"I'm not being a square. I just don't want to do drugs, OK?"

"Then go ahead Del baby. You do it and forget 'bout your crazy-ass old lady girlfriend."

"Shut your mouth, Bernadine. Del, don't take it. It makes you all crazy in the head and your start seeing scary things and you think you can fly like Superman and you jump off of buildings and die."

"Shush your foolish nonsense, girl."

"That's bullshit, Del. Only thing it'll do to you," explained Ritchie while the music oozed out of the speakers and spread across the walls and floors like a living creature, "is like to take you to a new reality. It'll expand your mind, man, dig what I mean?"

"Uh-huh," I nodded, my mouth slightly open.

Morning Star laughed at me. "That poor boy don't know what you talkin' 'bout, Ritchie L." She turned to face me. "He means, you'll take a trip and be everywhere and nowhere all at the same time."

"Like wherever you are, that's where it's at, man."

"Yeah, sugar, it helps you get away. Whenever it's gettin' to be too much, this helps you escape for a while. And then everythin's so nice."

"Escape?" I said. "From what?"

"From whatever's givin' you a heavy time. Whatever's bringin' you down, man. The war, the pigs, the establishment."

"Parents?" I asked.

"Yeah, man. Especially them."

"But what do you wanna escape from, Morning Star?"

"Oh sugar, that a long one," she said, smiling but not her usual big bright sensuous smile, but a subtler one with a hint of sadness in it. She thought for a moment, then said. "The city, for one."

"Huh?"

"Yeah. Ole badass Detroit. I'm talkin' the street, the ghetto. Somethin' you don't know about. Ooh, it's a mean town. Cold in the winter, hot and sticky in summer and rainy in between. Brothers and sisters out on the street, doin' all they business in front of everybody-- fightin', fuckin', stealin'--and the man just waitin' and watchin' your ass for one small wrong word and then they crackin' you upside your head. Mmm, mmm." she said shaking her head. "City just don't let you be. Everybody be hustlin', everybody be tryin' to stick it to the other to get a little cash in the hand. It ain't like that out here. Out here you can just relax, hang with the Beautiful People, get into the groove."

"Positive vibes, man. Positive vibes. Stop it now about all that negativity, Star. Don't bring me down. My trip's startin' and I don't want to be bummed out. Trip with me. Forget all that, come away and trip with me." Ritchie reached out and Morning Star placed her hand in his. He closed it tightly. "You trippin' yet, baby?"

"Yeah. It's happenin'."

"No negativity now, Star, or you'll trip bad. Get into the groove. Play that song again," said Ritchie to me or Ronni. "It's takin' me away." He was staring at something in front of him, his eyes wide.

I picked up the needle and the disc spun again, cold diamond hardness slicing into soft black.

Ronni took my hand and pulled. "C'mon," she said, "let's go outside." Absent-mindedly shoving the envelope into my pocket, I walked with her into the afternoon heat. Still holding hands, we strolled past the flowers, drooping under the white onslaught of heat, the bees and butterflies and flies hanging motionless in the molasses-thick air, waiting for a breeze that would never come.

I kept my hand tight around Ronni's, wondering at the ripples of tingling, electric waves traveling up my arm and shooting like little lightening bolts across my chest and into my stomach, my breath coming quick and shallow and the palms of my hands moist but warm. I had never held a girl's hand before.

"I don't like it when they do drugs like that," said Ronni, stooping to smell a daisy.

"But they like it."

"It's bad for you." We resumed walking. Her hand felt nice in mine.

"Doesn't seem to do them no--any--harm. They have fun."

"It probably messes with your mind or something. It's got to be unhealthy."

"How do you know, smarty pants?" I said. "Hey look--there goes a bluejay." The big bird flapped silently across the empty sky, rose higher and vanished into white glare.

Ronni stopped and stood in front of me. She picked up my other hand and held it. "Look, Del," she began, with that annoying adult look on her face, "I'm from Detroit. I know certain things about life that you don't."

"Oh, get outta here. I hate when you start talkin' like my mom."

"This place here Del, where you live, it's not real. You're up here in the bush in the hills and the nearest town's half-an-hour drive away and I don't even know where the nearest real city is."

"L.A. or San Francisco."

"How far are they?"

"Don't know."

"See what I mean?"

"No."

"You're cut off here. I'm from back east. From the city. I'm young but even I've seen things, Del. Lot's of bad things right before my own eyes. This ain't--isn't --life here. Detroit is life."

"You mean the stuff your sister was talkin' 'bout inside? 'Bout crime and shootin' people and riots and stuff?"

Ronni nodded. "Yes."

"Aw, I seen all that stuff a thousand times on TV."

"I've seen it for real. It's not the same as on TV," said Ronni, her eyes narrowing and her forehead creased by two deep wrinkles. "You can't smell or taste or feel things on TV. TV can't bleed."

"You're talkin' like my mom again."

There was a frozen second, and then it was almost like a dark cloth or a raven's wing lifted from Ronni's face. She smiled.

"Yeah," she said. "Maybe so. Still, it makes me sad to remember. Sometimes I don't want to go back."

"Go back? What do you mean?" My heart stopped beating.

"You know, at the end of summer."

136

"Oh yeah, right. But that's a long way off," I said, feeling the blood pulsating once again through my body.

"I hope so," smiled Ronni. "It's nice here. And it's nice with you, Del." Her smile, the sunny warmth dripping over us from above as we held hands in a yard of flowers, Ronni now stepping nearer, me sensing the heat steaming from the palms of her hands gripping mine, entwining with the heat rising up in waves from her body, the low dreamy hum of bees, Ronni's eyes like bright stars in the heavy, scented air as I felt an immense tugging, a thick velvet rope sunk into my chest and me falling forward.

"Well?" said Ronni, looking at me and still smiling.

"Well what?"

"Well, silly, aren't you going to kiss me?" she said, closing her eyes and lifting her chin.

"Oh, yeah, sure." My heart now thumping tremendously at the top of my throat, lava blood splashing against the inside of my skull, I leaned forward unsteadily, stepped on Ronni's foot, mumbled "Sorry," then leaned again, pursed my lips and pressed them against hers, my eyes wide open in terror and amazement and bliss. It all ended with a loud smack.

I coughed, cleared my throat and scratched behind my ear. Then I started grinning like a stupid goof.

"Wow," was all I could say.

12

The next two nights I dreamt about Ronni and how her hands had felt in mine, her bright eyes and fine soft lips, her lovely kiss and the inexplicable hypnotic heat broiling off her body. In the mornings I'd wake up as stiff as in iron rod, aching all over until I eased it away with a few firm jerks of my hand bringing me into that spasmodic, oily, writhing second of warmth and velvety blindness. But the feeling would always come back in a couple hours time and I'd do it in the bush or behind the barn or standing over the toilet or sitting alone in the living room watching TV. But always that feeling returned. It was good.

Maybe the summer wasn't so bad after all. I thought about what Ronni had said, about this land not being real life, and I guessed she was right but I didn't care. It wasn't all bad in the house on our own in the middle of the thick chaparral in the eternal sunshine in an unending summer. Maybe I liked it that way. Maybe I didn't yet want what was inevitably coming. Maybe I just wanted to bask in my golden, hilly isolation, away from complications.

I hadn't been to the town since school got out and as the day of the party approached and my mom made frequent trips down the long hill into the town to buy food and drink, I declined to come along. I didn't want to run into any of my fellow students or teachers at the shopping center nor drive past the school or the corner grocery store where the big kids hung out smoking cigarettes and drinking out of brown lunch bags and telling dirty jokes. Maybe if I stayed away from all that, I figured, I'd disappear or be forgotten and could live out the rest of my days happy on the ranch with Ronni and Ritchie Lane and Morning Star, Cochise and Duke. I wouldn't need much more than that.

The Monster and I weren't looking forward to the coming party. It would mean lots and lots of big people talking about boring stuff and drinking and piling huge shovelfulls of steaming meat and salad into their greasy red faces. It would mean that alky Kay Lifton-Wright and her weird daughter and Al Wainwright and his creepy sons. And as the Big Day grew near, my mom and dad started getting more and more on each other's nerves, and small heated battles took place like when my dad announced that Mary Ellen and I should play in the middle of the yard while the party was going on so that the grown ups could watch us and be amused. "It'll set a hell of a nice mood," he explained. My mom lowered her head at him and chewed on something in her mouth. "That," she said, "is the most ridiculous thing I've ever heard."

"I want them kids out there. It makes a good feelin' in the air, y'know a summery evenin' kinda thing. Ya got your drink in your hand, jazz in the air, kids over in the flowers playin' 'n shit. It's classy."

"Absolutely not. I will not have our children used like some sort of cheap prop for your collection of drunken friends to observe."

"Goddamn it!" exploded my dad, smashing his fist on the kitchen table top, "These kids are gonna do what I say."

My mom glared at him, her mouth tight. She spoke each word distinctly, with razor-sharp clarity. "If you force the children to act like animals in a zoo tomorrow night, you had better find yourself another party organizer because I will not be around."

My dad's steely blue eyes narrowed at my mom standing at the stove with a large wooden spoon in one hand, eyes black and sizzling.

"Shit," he said after a long, thick pause. "Have it your own god dammed way. Hell if I care." And my dad poured himself another gin but instead of drinking it, sort of stared into for a while.

Personally, it didn't matter to me how we were to be placed or used or worked during the party, because I had a Secret Weapon that I was planning to use that would help me to escape from what was most likely going to be a boring evening. There wasn't any party for me anyway if Ronni couldn't be there and I still hated my dad for being the way he was about people like Morning Star and Ronni, and I was still angry with my mom for allowing my dad's lunatic opinions to set the mood of the house. My mom and dad didn't know that I hated them, though, because on the outside--should they care to notice, which they didn't--I liked them, but on the inside I had made deep, indelible notes to myself on the pliable tissue of my brain, and I inside myself knew exactly what was wrong and what right and I would never, ever forget it. Never ever.

Davy never called me back so I was going to be alone in the party for sure, which made the idea of my Secret Weapon even more enticing. Kathy had lucked out--or perhaps my parents had decided to appease her--and she was allowed to invite her boyfriend Ernie and a couple more of her friends. So she was going to be able to enjoy a party within the party. When you're big you always get what you want.

As each passing day was warmer and sunnier and brighter and longer than the last, I hung outdoors a lot, playing with Cochise. It was still very hot, but the heat wave had broken, shattering the apocalyptic predictions of the local farmers and ranchers. Cochise was growing into a healthy pup, with alert, intelligent eyes and a bouncy, friendly personality. He was smart, too. Whenever I'd whistle in a certain tone or would call his name, he'd know exactly that it was me and would stop whatever he was doing and come tearing out at me with a happy look on his face. A dog, when he is loved and well and content, will smile; and Cochise was the smilingest dog I'd ever seen. He was always happy and I was happy with him. We were pals.

Saturday morning started off like an afternoon: a severe white sun in a burning pale blue cloudless sky, no wind and no shadow anywhere. It was so hot all the dogs sought out the shadowed spots inside the pole barn or underneath my mom's car. The Monster and I stayed indoors, playing quietly in our rooms or fighting over the TV. Towards late afternoon, my mom told me to water down the plants in the yard because they had taken such a beating from the sun all day long.

The garden hose was hot and felt melted in my hand, and only spurted out hot water: it took a couple of minutes of running full out until the water cooled. When I turned the hose on the flowers and the grass they looked pretty sad-- pale and thin and limp and shriveled. As the water splashed over the dusty ground and the thirsty plants, you could almost hear them drinking. I placed my thumb on the nozzle, partially blocking the gurgling water and a fine stream of liquid arched out in a thin fan, cool mist hanging in the air and sprinkling my face with soft kisses. Two white butterflies flittered overhead and I immediately put on my steel helmet and flak jacket and crouched down into a foxhole and, aiming the machine gun skywards, fired great quivering gobs of translucence towards the fleeting shapes, tiny droplets exploding onto white powdery wings.

"Del!"

My body jumped, and the hose sprung out of my and lay writhing on the ground, bleeding and alive.

"Del!" called my mom from the kitchen window, "Come in here and help me, will you?"

"Comin'!" I grabbed the green snake spitting silver blood and squeezed it to death then, as it still dripped venom, coiled it around my arm and laid it near the faucet.

Stepping into the kitchen, I drew in a deep breath. "Wow. Smell's great. Can't wait to start eatin'!"

Steel pots covered the stove, some with wooden handles sticking out of them, others obscured in steam and topped by chattering lids. The counter was littered with opened jars of spices, peeled cloves of garlic and sliced onions, a wedge of Parmesan cheese and a grater and a large broad-bladed knife. The oven light was on and I could feel the heat radiating off it. My mom, wearing a white t-shirt and khaki pants, wild veins of hair jungling her face, spun away from the refrigerator to face me, at the same time kicking the door shut with her foot. With a delicate deft motion, she brushed a lock of hair from her eyes.

"Here," she said, handing me an armful of carrots, celery, lettuce and tomatoes and green onions, "wash these, please, and cut everything up. This too." She set an avocado on top of the pile.

I dumped the vegetables into the sink and ran water over them. Then I took the large knife off the counter, picked up the avocado and sliced clean around it, like a surgeon opening a skull.

"Once the salad's made," sighed my mom. "That'll be about it."

I pulled apart the two halves of the avocado and plunged the tip of the knife into the big greenish-black seed inside which stared up at me like an eye. "How many are gonna come tonight?"

"Too many." My mom poured herself a tall glass of orange juice from the pitcher in the refrigerator. "This is the last big party we give. I'm sick of all this preparing."

With a large spoon in one hand, I began scooping out the firm, green flesh and let it plop onto the counter. "Diced or sliced?" I asked.

My mom turned and faced me, brushed the hair out of her eyes with the hand holding the glass and looked at the counter. "Diced."

"Should we fire up the barbeque now to get the briquettes hot?" The steel blade of the knife sank through the greenness, clicking on the cool Formica counter.

"No, god no. Your father would have a king-sized fit if we did that. That's his baby, so he can deal with it. I'm not in the mood for one of his screaming rages." My mom wiped another strand of hair from her eyes, which immediately fell back to where it had been. "I'm not in the mood for anything any more."

Slanting the broad edge of the knife, I slid it along the slick counter top, gathered up the cubed green flesh and dumped it into a large salad bowl sitting on the table. With the knife upraised in one hand, I advanced to the sink. "I'll just cut up the rest of them," I said.

"Fine," said my mom. "I'm going to get ready." And she left the room, turning off the stove as she passed by it.

I had just finished chopping up the vegetables when I heard the pickup truck pull into the driveway, the door slam and my dad's brisk, weighty footsteps crunching nearer. Then the kitchen door burst open.

"Jesus H. Christ, it's hotter'n a sonofabitch out there. Where's your mom?" He laid a bundle of white paper stained with deep red blotches on the table.

"She's gettin' ready."

"What's that?" said my dad.

"In the bedroom," I said in a near shout to his good ear, "Gettin' dressed."

"Oh. Get me some ice and a slice of lemon, Del, and put it in a glass. Christ, I need a drink."

I handed the glass to my dad and he mixed in one part tonic water and three parts gin, took a long drink and let out a sigh of contentment. That first sip of gin at the end of the day, I realized, listening to the ice crack and tinkle against the glass, was what pulled my dad through his long, hard hours of work. That first drink almost made him happy.

I pointed with the knife. "What's in the paper?"

"Cut off head. Heh!--just pullin' your leg, Del. That's eats for tonight. Steaks and ribs and pork chops from Henry's down the hill. Christ almighty, I done near and forgot--there's ice and beer and cases of wine in the bed of the pickup. Go fetch it and bring it out back. Dump the ice in a trashcan and put the beer on to chill. I better start up with the barbecue. Before you know it, them sonofabitches gonna start arrivin'."

I went outside to the truck and looked at everything stacked up in the bed. When my parents did something, they did it in a grand style. If twenty people were invited, they'd cook and have drinks for sixty. My dad always said treat your guests like kings and show 'em we ain't no poor ignorant Oakies eatin' biscuits 'n gravy. When I asked my mom about this, she explained that the one thing my dad feared was being penniless, something he had experienced during the Great Depression. That's why he always kept a thick bundle of twenty-dollar bills rolled up in his pocket.

I rested my hand on the truck's swing-down door but pulled it instantly away. The steel was burning hot from the sun. I figured I'd better start on the bags of cubed ice first, before it all melted. These I carried four at a time--one under each arm, one in each hand--to the back yard where my dad had wheeled out the giant iron barbecue he had welded together out of scrap metal. Blue flames licked up from within its deep interior. My dad sat on a wooden bench he had built last year from spare planks of redwood. His shoulders slouched as he stared into the flames, blue fire mirrored in the blue marble eyes, his elbows resting on his knees, the rough red hands dangling. He looked old and tired: he was both. Late afternoon shadows crept into the lines cut across his forehead, lines etched under his eyes, shadows filling up the hollows in the sagging skin of his neck. In the reflected fire his gray hair flashed silver, and silver eyebrows hooded the fiery blue of the tired, staring eyes.

I hauled the rest of the ice and the cases of bottled beer out of the truck, then poured clattering bags of ice into a big, plastic green garbage can, set a layer of beer onto it, covered it with more ice and laid another row of bottles on that and so on until it was filled.

Then my dad sent me out to the pole barn to get the fold-up chairs and tables which I--alone--set up in the yard as the afternoon bled away; the day was fading but the warmth, a sticky, clinging warmth, stayed. When I was at last finished, rivulets of sweat streaking down my forearms and back and down from my temples, I gulped in the thick air, trying to catch my breath. I felt angry and misused. I was always the idiot who had to set everything up while the others, wherever they were, got to screw around enjoying themselves. I guess my mood reflected in my face because my dad looked up at me, laughed and said, "Have one of them beers, Del. That'll hold you. Now you're gettin' to be a man, you gotta learn to work just like your old man. Go ahead, have one of 'em. You done earned it."

"Um, OK," I said, a bit surprised and bewildered. My dad had never offered me anything to drink before and it felt kind of weird. It made me think of how everyone kept saying things like, "You're not a kid anymore" or "You're getting to be a man, Del," which was strange to hear. I didn't feel what they apparently saw. It was the same old me in the mirror, except for a couple of lonely hairs on my chin, the same Del that had always stared back at me out of the mirror. I didn't see the change.

I went over to the big green trashcan and plunged my hand into the ice: the shock was instantly refreshing and the cold drew all heat and weariness out of my body. The beer bottle I yanked up was pearled with drops of water and very cold. With an opener that lay nearby, I popped the lid, tilted the bottle and drank of my first beer. It was fizzy, bitter and left an aftertaste in my mouth of flavors I had never experienced before; I wasn't sure if I liked it. Turning the bottle slowly in my hand, I gazed at its bowling pin shape and looked at the label.

"Don't read the damn thing. Drink it," called my dad, laughing.

I drank some more, opening and closing my mouth rapidly to get the taste. It tasted grown up. This was one more of the mysterious adult things that kept happening to me this summer, and here I was doing it right in front of my dad. It almost felt as if I should be hiding, taking secret sips with Davy behind the barn, or in the bathrooms at school or out behind the bleachers or late at night at the beach. But here I was in my own back yard, drinking a tall cold one. Far out, I said in my mind. Far out.

"Hot damn," said my dad. "What a sight."

Looking up, I saw my mom emerging from the kitchen.

"You look like a million bucks," my dad exclaimed.

She was dressed in black pocketless pants that were tight at the ankles, and a silky, silvery-white blouse. Her dark hair was carefully brushed and pulled back in a ponytail and golden earrings gleamed from each ear. Her dark brown eyes looked lush against the sky's deep blue.

"You look great, mom," I said, and catching the look in her eyes, quickly added, "Dad said I could have one."

"Boy's old enough. He worked like a regular s.o.b. settin' everythin' up."

"Only one," said my mom, frowning slightly.

Before she could reconsider, I slipped past her and took my beer into the living room, where I found this week's *Life* lying on the sofa. Sipping from the bottle, I flipped through its pages, drawn automatically to a photo essay about the war. The brief text explained how we were killing more of them than they of us, but from the black and white photos of young soldiers with ancient, empty eyes, nude burning children with flailing arms, wizened peasants squatting under straw hats behind sheets of flames, and the dead, the dead with dark stains on their shirts and pants, the dead of blank fish eyes, the dead of them and of us, sprawled alone in the jungle, heaped into piles like chopped wood: all this said that nobody was winning this war. Everybody looked like losers to me.

I switched on the TV. The news, and more positive reports from the war. Maybe we were winning it. Who cared? Who could tell? They showed clips of fighter jets streaking the sky with white-tailed missiles and the jungle exploding orange and red in their wake. They showed

VC being rounded up by screaming soldiers with bayonets at the ends of their M16s. They showed a general with a square, honest chin reviewing a long line of dead VC, limbs contorted, chins jutting, barefoot and half naked and the general with the square U.S. Grade A chin looked grimly into the camera that he always seemed to know was there, and spoke about the many battles he had won and how we really were winning the war.

Finishing the beer, I reached out and switched off the TV.

I sat very still in the big chair for awhile, mind blank, mouth open, gazing into the void of the gray-green TV screen, my body sinking wonderfully into the seat cushions, my head spinning in gentle, pleasant revolutions. Presently, I became aware of a car heading up our road, headlights silvering through the twilight, and Duke started barking. Rising up, I headed to the kitchen to see which guest was the first to arrive. Involuntarily, my hand stroked the Secret Weapon in my pocket. Not now, I whispered to myself. Later when I really need it. When things get boring and the grown ups loud or when Al Wainwright's sons started picking on me, then I'd do it.

Through the screen door leading to the kitchen, I watched Eddie McGhee and is wife Marge getting out of their beat-up and rusty old pickup. Eddie had on his usual cap and blue shirt and baggy work pants, but instead of work boots he wore a pair of old sneakers: I guess he thought he'd better dress up for the party. Marge, a huge woman with massive breasts and roller-curled hair, three chins, pudgy bags of fat swinging from under her arms and a pug nose, looked even huger than usual in her light yellow dress with tiny green flowers printed on it.

"Hey dere sonny boy," grinned Eddie as the couple pushed in past me. "Where da folks?"

"Back yard," I said, jerking my thumb over my shoulder. I followed them outside.

Eddie and Marge made straight for the beer and, beers clutched firmly in their hands, headed for a nearby table filled with chips, dips and a big bowl of salsa. Eddie tilted his bottle up and took a along swig; Marge filled a paper plate full of food and shoved a handful potato chips into her face. She chewed with her mouth open, giving us all a good look at the sticky mush inside.

"Hey dere, Johnny," said Eddie, moving over to where my dad stood at the barbecue. "Birthday boy. Ya feel any older?"

"Hell no. I don't never feel no age. I'm as young and strong as a draft horse and horny as a stallion."

All three laughed, Marge's breasts and belly shaking like a dish of Jell-O. A blob of pulverized potato chip and salsa shot out of her cavernous mouth and landed on her chin. With a delicate swipe of her pinky, she scooped it off and deposited it on her tongue. "Christ, Johnny," she giggled, "ain't you a funny'n."

My dad winked at her, took a drink from his glass and speared a raw steak from off a platter with a long, thin two-pronged fork. With a violent hiss it hit the grill and was soon joined by several more. Through the sizzling roar of the meat, my mom, followed by Kay Lifton-Wright and her daughter, stepped into the yard.

"Hello, Kay," said my dad in his Charming Host voice which he usually used at the beginning of parties before the real drinking started. "How the hell are you?"

"John," said Kay, a glass perched dramatically in one hand as she floated across the flowers and bricks to my dad. "Happy birthday to you." From her easy, slightly sexy smile and the calmness and smoothness with which she moved, I knew she had started her drinking already. One look into her swimmy eyes confirmed it.

Wanda, thin and pasty in a sleeveless pale green summer dress that would have clung to her body if there were a body to cling to, came up to me. Instinctively, my hand pressed against the Secret Weapon in my pocket. Zero Hour was fast approaching.

"Hello, Del."

"Hi."

"Funny to see you out here with the grown ups and all."

"Whaddaya mean?"

"I mean, I thought you'd be playing with your toys in your room, like a baby," Wanda, wearing a thin wire smile dangling on the outter part of her face, spread her arms out and twirled in front of me, the bottom of her dress lifting to reveal dead white sticks in yellow socks underneath.

"Maybe I don't play with toys no more."

Wanda continued twirling. "Ha! That'll be the day."

"Don't believe me then."

"I don't. And anyways what would you possibly do if you didn't like toys anymore?"

"Stuff."

"What stuff?"

"I drank a beer today."

"Big deal. That's small fry stuff," said Wanda, that thin wire smile still stretched across her face.

"And I know this girl."

Wanda suddenly stopped her twirling. Eyes narrowed, she extended her head out on the end of her long, skinny neck and peered at me. "You got a girlfriend, Del?"

My face began burning. "Maybe so, maybe not. Don't be so nosey all the time."

"I'm not. I couldn't care less really. I don't know any girl dumb enough to have such a stupid boyfriend like you." She started twirling again. "Anyway, I got three boyfriends and we go to movies together and my mother let's them come over sometimes and they fight over me."

"So what?" I rolled my eyes.

"And," said Wanda, standing in front of me now with her hands on her hips, "We kiss."

"Whoopee."

"You're just jealous because you've never kissed a girl and never will because you're so ugly."

"Oh, I don't know," I said, trying to sound mysterious and bored at the same time. I figured shoving both hands into my pants pockets would help, so I did. "Maybe you shouldn't be such a smarty-pants. Maybe I have kissed a girl." I sauntered past Wanda, who watched me go by with her arms dangling limply at her sides and her mouth partially open. "Bye-bye," I smiled as creepily as I could. "I gotta go to the can," and I slipped into the kitchen. Before Wanda could follow, I had raced through the kitchen and was outside, running to the pole barn. I looked in the doghouse, but could see no sign of Taffy or the puppies, which was odd. Moving into the barn, I stopped, listened and called out, "Cochise!" After several seconds, there was a familiar yelp and Cochise toddled out from underneath one of the trucks. I knelt down and rubbed his soft head. "Hey boy," I whispered, "where ya been hidin'? Where's the rest of the family?" I called for Duke and Taffy, but they did not appear. That was normal, though, because at this time--early evening--the big dogs liked to go off into the hills and chase the rabbits and quail which came out to feed in the coolness. But where were the rest of the puppies? I wondered.

Keeping to the shadows of the barn so as not to be seen, I played with Cochise and watched our driveway fill up with station wagons and pickup trucks and sedans as the guests arrived. Ernie drove up with a car full of teens and Kathy emerged from her room and greeted him with a long kiss, open-mouthed just like Morning Star and Ritchie Lane did it. I watched Ernie put his hand on my sister's butt and leave it there. Then came an old U.S. army jeep driven by a huge, powerfully built man with curly hair and a full, bushy beard. Al Wainwright. I pressed my back against the cold corrugated steel interior wall of the barn and listened to the heavy clump of Al and his three sons as they marched into the house.

Now was the time. Reaching into my pocket, I pulled out a white envelope, opened it and looked at the strange white stamp that Ritchie Lane had given me a few days before. The Secret Weapon. It didn't look like much, really, so I picked it up, sniffed it and looked at it from different angles. Then I shrugged, closed my eyes and opened my mouth like I had seen Morning Star do, and placed the stamp on my extended tongue. As it dissolved innocently in my mouth, I kept my eyes closed, waiting for something amazing to happen. It didn't. Slightly disappointed, I decided to return to the party. I was getting hungry and wanted to get some of the ribs before the guests devoured them.

Setting Cochise down, I had just started to leave the barn when I caught sight of one of the puppies hiding behind a truck tire. Moist eyes gleaming brown out of the surrounding dark. I whistled softly through my teeth and said, "C'mere boy," but the pup would not show himself. Then I picked up a chip of wood and held it out to him as if it were food. His nose appeared out of the shadows, then the rest of his face, as he walked on unsteady legs towards the wood, sniffing. At that moment I noticed something strange. Flecks of white foam hung from the corners of the pup's mouth and he wobbled as he walked, his head trembling slightly. Milky fluid ran from his eyes and nose. Just then I heard howling, long pained cries coming from the surrounding hills. Night descended rapidly, springing up from the dancing fathomless shadows of the barn, which seemed to be alive. A chill went down my spine and the night suddenly transformed into a menacing black thing, creeping towards me. The little puppy was now sniffing my hand and I yanked it away. But then I felt sorry for him, patted him on the head and picked him up and carried him to the water dish. I had the impression that something in the dark was watching me and I kept glancing over my shoulder to peer into the shifting, dusky formlessness in which I could see nothing. I heard the howling again as I set the pup before the water and watched him twitch his nose at it, then turn away. More howls broke out in the night, coming from several different directions at once and, with a last glance at the puppy, I hurried back to the party in the back yard.

By now I was starting to feel a little funny. I guess I was just hungry. But I felt nervous and slightly jumpy, like I was about to get in trouble for something or like I was expecting someone or something. And then I started to giggle. It could have been something I overheard from a guest or an expression on someone's face, but it was so funny I couldn't help but giggle. Then the giggling itself became funny and I giggled even more, my body feeling rubbery and loose.

Now things where starting to appear to me in startling detail and I was seeing normal things in ways I had never seen them before. The sizzling of the steaks and ribs filled my ears and I strolled over to where my dad stood, slowly turning the meat, squirting water at the fat-fed flames if they rose too high, talking to some guy in a white shirt with a round red face sitting in a fold-up chair and drinking gin from a clear glass. I found it amazing how light was caught by the crystal of the glass and then radiated out with brilliance in blues and reds. Stepping up to the big barbeque, I peered over its side at the browning meat inside, striped black from the grill, tears of fat hissing on the gray white briquettes below, the air warm and wonderful from the smell of roasting meat and garlic salt. My eyes zoomed in on the briquettes, a living world of smoke and fire, spitting ash, lashing out with blue tongues, shifting one under the other, some briquettes partially black and well defined, others soft and dusty, with beating red glowing hearts visible through crevices in their bodies, others crumbling into soft puffs of powder, thin primordial wisps of smoke curling up from the ruins in waves.

"You hear me?"

A voice rose out of the fire.

"Del. You want some or not? What the hell's matter with ya?"

The voice flew above my head and following it, I looked up to see where it had landed. Through the smoke and fire, my dad's red faced glowed fiercely at me.

"What?" I said, feeling as if I was slowly emerging from thick, sucking gelatin into a type of clarity.

"You gone deaf? I said, what are ya havin'? Steak or ribs or both?"

"Ribs."

"Christ, that's the last time I let the kid have a beer," laughed my dad to the guy holding the radiating glass of gin. He handed me a paper plate piled with steaming pork ribs. I carried this to the edge of the brick terrace, to just where the flowers crawled up from the deepness within the darkened yard. Things were beginning to get interesting. Weird. Suddenly I was sitting down, although I could not remember sitting down or even deciding to sit down, and a rib was in my mouth, but I had not put it there. I think. While figuring this out, my mouth began to chew, and it was amazing. The rib, I mean. How it just got there, and I chewed. That was incredible, too, chewing, chewing the meat in my mouth, the fine fibers of flesh, the tearing, the mashing, the machine gun burst of flavors--each with a special color of its own--and a noise, feeling every loose piece alone and floating in my mouth. "Wow," I think I said.

I heard a loud rustling above my head and to one side and I looked up at a tree. It was shimmering softly, silvery and I smiled. Frowning, I watched two leaves brushing against each other, *crrrrr crrrrrr crrrrrrr*. It was a silveriness, a humming moonly silveriness and the

151

incredibleness of the brushing together of the leaves that made me watch, stupefied, for hours.

Another outburst of laughter and I turned my head, feeling my head rotating on the steel ball bearing in my neck and in the turning everything flashing brilliant red. Raised voices. Tinkling glass. Laughter. Pants' legs swishing. Steel high heels clicking on the brick. A sudden burst of red and everyone instantly froze: a head thrown back, mouth wide open, white teeth; a bottle of beer poised before pink lips; two ice people not chatting; hands and arms and feet suspended. Then a black and white flash from a light bulb on a camera from 1934 in an old news reel and I was looking at frozen gray newspaper photos from *Life*, this life: nude child screaming, her body on fire; camouflage pants on the legs of a young black man in a pool of black blood in mud; unmoving jets pinned to a gray sky above a jungle exploding into white and gray clouds.

"Hey," I said.

In an instant came a roaring rush of mingled party sounds and life bursting into my head, all motion and noise and stinks and touches. Colors everywhere. Reds and yellows and purples and blues, turquoise of shirts and dresses, pink of faces, golden on shoes, all vibrant, deeply rich, pulsating alive in color. I loved watching them move. Such happiness. "Oh, yeah," I nodded, "I know," and I smiled broadly, watching.

The meat on my paper plate was moving. Not shaking, but stretching, elongating. Long and brown and charred at the edges, a rib crawled over to a rib, which expanded and lengthened itself, then wormed to the other side of the plate. I couldn't eat this stuff. It was alive.

I decided to get up and thought some more, then decided to get up and I knew in my head that I had decided to get up and so I thought it'd be OK--really--to get up and I decided that I guess I'd get up. Then I started to get worried. What if I got up and everybody saw me getting up and then knew about me, about what I'd done and I'd be up and they'd all be laughing at me and my mom and dad would kill me many thousands of times over if they knew.

I decided to get up.

Up, and I was standing and it was alright but I knew I'd have to keep cool and not freak out and not let anybody know or they'd kill me. I tried to whistle but my mouth was amazingly dry and then I had a powerful sensation that my mom was staring at me, so I narrowed my eyes and sank my head between my shoulders and carefully, very carefully, looked around, spying. My mom wasn't watching me. Anymore. So maybe it was OK and nobody really knew. I'd have to play it really cool to not get busted with what I'd done and somehow I felt myself emerging from myself and where I'd been and I now knew that I could look, act and talk like everything was just normal. Normal.

Once normal, my senses were hit by a massive amount of noise and light, harshly loudly, disharmonious. I turned, saw a greenness in the night at a tree and near it was Wanda. The greenness, not the night or the tree. I decided to walk up to her and be normal.

She was standing with her legs apart and her head tilted and she had no arms. Okeydokey, no arms, I thought to myself. I tapped her on the shoulder. "Hi, Wanda," I said in an extremely normal voice. "How are you?"

With really unbelievable speed, she faced me, a red smear of lipstick slashed where her lips had once been, and her chin.

"What?"

"Scram, buttwipe." My eyes enlarged and I nearly screamed but at the last second I realized the essence of the head behind Wanda. Be normal.

"Hey, Hank," I said. It was Al Wainwright's oldest son. Really.

"Fuck off," Hank growled. He was nineteen, mustached, wrinkled on his forehead, and mean-eyed.

"Yeah, go away you weirdo and play with your toys like a little boy," said the wire on Wanda's mouth. "We're busy."

She turned, placed her arms around Hank's log neck, cocked her neck at a strange angle and he reached up with his hand.

Still being normal, I returned to the party.

Walking into the harshness of light and sound again, I passed by Eddie McGhee, sitting in a chair with a beer in his hand. He sat with his knees apart and his head bowed. His eyes were red and the size of glass basketballs. "Hey dere, boy," he said, raising an arm up that was

153

apparently too heavy because it dropped like a stone to his side. Eddie's wife was in the middle of a small group of laughing people. The paper plate in her chubby hand sagged in the center under the weight of steaks and ribs and garlic bread and a small heap of potato salad.

And I was being normal and a spy and nobody still knew what I'd done. I saw my dad talking with Al Wainright. Mr. Knows-it-all, Mr. College Eddication, my dad sometimes called him. Al was big and hairy and he had a very deep, booming voice. He had studied, so he claimed, architecture and engineering at Berkeley, but he said his teachers were all lying bastards so he dropped out and, because the government was full of lying bastards as well, he dropped out of America, too, and lived with his sons in a cabin in the hills and they didn't go to school and never paid taxes.

"Al you're a lyin' sonofabitch," my dad was laughing. "You never said nothin' 'bout back east before."

"I sure as hell did," boomed Al, pausing long enough to take a sip of beer. "Ask Sarah if you're too drunk to remember."

My dad looked around, then called out "Sarah! C'mere."

My mom left a small group of eating, drinking partiers and walked up to my dad's side. "Sarah," said my dad, "help me show Al here up as a lyin' s.o.b. He ain't never told us he gone to Harvard, did he?"

"Yes, he told us that a while back, don't you remember Johnny? You were there for a year, weren't you Al?"

"Shit," said my dad.

"Nine months."

"Then they throwed your ass out."

"Hell no!" shouted Al. "I left. Bunch of ignorant bastards. Didn't know jack shit about anything. Never seen a larger group of incompetents in my life."

Without another word, my mom slipped away from the two men. I caught Al's eyes watching her go.

"Tell me somethin', Al. If you're so damn smart, why you always quitin' jobs or gettin' throwed outta places? What's the matter, can't get a-goin' when the goin' gets hot?"

"Har har!" barked Al, and he slapped my dad on his broad back, ham-sized hand smashing into solid steel. I turned from them then, leaving them glaring at each others' full, red faces, reeking of alcohol and smoke, muscles in their necks bulging with rage-filled life, eyes unblinking and stony.

I decided to head outside to see what Kathy and her friends were up to, but the more I concentrated on reaching the door, the farther away it was. I'd stare for hours at someone's nose. I listened to the sound of my own breathing for a long time. I felt a slight breeze passing through my head. Then, in a corner near the door, I saw a silvery gray cat sitting, its silky body expanding as it drew in each breath. Crouching down, I watched it. I couldn't see its face, only front paws and the plush cushion of its body. I crept forward, wanting to sink my hand into it because I knew it would feel good.

"Jesus Christ, stop screwin' around, Del. I almost ran right over you."

As I drew near, I stood up to look normal and approached the corner. The cat had disappeared. I retreated a couple of steps and the animal reappeared, so I moved forward again. It vanished. This went on for several minutes, or hours or days. Then there was a sharp volley of laughter coming from somewhere behind which threw me into a flash of clarity and I stood up, straight and tall, patted down my hair and tucked in my shirttails and, striding over to the corner I realized all at once that there had never been a cat. I had been watching a shadow.

More laughter and a wave of paranoia swept across me. Had everybody been watching me act like an idiot? I didn't dare turn around. Instead, I tried to grip my mind around the still flashing clarity and, my back held straight, arms hanging at my sides and my legs swinging underneath, I carried myself out the door, floated through the kitchen and into the driveway, filled with the humped black shapes of cars and trucks, stranded and dying like beached whales. Inside my head, my brain collapsed and turned to soft butter. I stared upwards at the wheeling stars.

A distant red glowing pin-sized comet or star or planet dropped down towards the horizon, hovered, rose, glowed with a burst of energy, traveled and glowed hotly again. It was so close, so close. Arms extended outwards, I moved towards it.

"Hey, runt." A heavy South American python dropped from a jungle tree and wrapped around my neck, squeezing. My neck bent under the weight and there was a hard, bony rapping on the top of my skull.

"Ow." I said calmly. "Lemmie go."

"Beat it, shrimp." Laughter fell out of the sky.

"Goddamn you Del, you better not tell."

"He tells, he dies."

"Lemmie go, snake."

"What he say?"

"I'll kill 'im for sure." More laughter, coming now from the tiny glowing star. The light pulsating off it suddenly revealed a face.

"Ow. Let go of me," I said firmly to the python.

"Aw, let 'im go. He'll start cryin'."

The snake slithered away and I unbent myself and blinked into the night.

"Stop starin' you dumbshit."

"Yeah and shut your mouth. You look like a retard."

"Who is this kid anyway?"

"My brother."

"Jeez. When was the accident?" Another explosion of laughter.

Suddenly, faces were popping out of the nightness all over the place. I saw Kathy's face, and Ernie's and a couple of faces I didn't know and a couple more I knew but I didn't know the names that belong to the faces. They were all laughing so I started laughing, too.

"Hey," I said in all normalness. The red burning thing was now sticking out of Kathy's face. She took it in her hand and floated it to a girl with long blond hair sitting next to her inside the bed of a pickup truck where they were all sitting. The girl with the redness sucked in air.

"Your bro's a trip, Kat. Hey kid, wanna hit?"

"Wanna hit who?" I asked, a question which was received with a thunderclap of laughter.

"Too much," said someone.

"The kid's stoned, man," said an unfamiliar woman's voice.

"Beat it," said a face that I knew belonged to the face of Lee, Al Wainwright's youngest son. "No kids allowed."

"Don't gotta beat it if I don't wanna."

"Go beat your meat," giggled Ernie.

"Sit on it and rotate," threw in another and there was more laughter.

"You guys are loonies," was my comeback, and I turned around and headed indoors again.

I was having longer and longer periods of normalness again and I wondered if I was coming back from wherever it was I had been. I felt exhausted, not so much in my brain which was still charged with nervous energy, but in my body which was heavy with a profound weariness. I couldn't shake the feeling that I was being watched or laughed at or followed, and I cut my eyes and watched the shifting shadows with suspicion. The back yard was crowded and a party-roar, like the sea, crashed into my ears. I was sleepy and wide-awake at the same time, and alternately felt relaxed and wired.

Suddenly, there was the popping crash of broken glass and a deep man's voice said "What the fuck--?." Looking up, I saw my dad, his whole body stiff and as tightly wound as a spring, leaning into Al Wainright's bearded face.

"I seen that you sonofabitch."

"I don't know what the --"

"You keep your fuckin' hands off my wife you cocksucker."

"Johnny, he merely touched my shoulder," said my mom. Everybody had stopped talking and was watching the two men. The surrounding silence was painful.

"I seen what he done."

"You're drunk," sneered Al.

"Not that drunk, I ain't."

"Johnny, don't you dare start anything," said my mom, arms folded, her face bloodless and white, hanging in the night's sky.

"This fucker's started this shit," hissed my dad, never taking his unblinking eyes off of Al.

"I sure as hell don't need to put up with this uncouth bastard's antics," said Al, placing his broad hand on my dad's chest as he

157

attempted to walk past him.

That's all it took. There was a blur of pink motion, Al spinning in the silver sheen of the backyard lights, my mom screaming "No!" with her open hands on her cheeks, Al floating gently down to the red brick floor and my dad's blue eyes fired with a yellow flame inside the hard, unmelting ice. And everywhere, the awful, empty silence of the night that made me want to cry from the beauty of it.

13

I think it was that the unnormalness hit me again and I sort of flew or floated or was pushed along by some kind of breeze that lifted my feet up a few inches from the floor and then I was in my room. The trip passed and I knew with a reasonable amount of certainty that I was me in my very own room again. I remembered my leaving the party, Al's sudden weird desire to lay on his back on the bricks with his arms spread out, my mom freaking out and screaming and my dad, his gray-silver hair askew, breathing hard out of his mouth and his eyes burning like diamonds in a red sea. Or was that just part of the trip, too?

I didn't know. All I knew was that I was exhausted. And nervous. My hands shook and my feet would have started tap dancing if they had known how to. Tightly stretched guitar strings ran from the center of my chest to my legs and arms and I knew that one more twist on the crank inside my head would make them snap. I had an enormous desire to giggle, and to cry. But neither giggle nor tear would come, no matter how hard I tried to make them. God, was I tired. I wanted it all to end so that I could fall asleep for about a hundred years.

I stripped off all my clothes and lay on top of the covers on my bed. But the minute I shut my eyes, my heart started racing, my hands and feet began moving and my breath quickened. I had a chest-feeling-- not a brain-knowing--that something was about to happen. I felt tense, strung up, and weary. Shutting my eyes again, I tried filling my revving brain with pictures of Ronni and Ritchie Lane and Morning

Star. When these flashed by, I looked at Cochise, then the Monster and Kathy, then my parents, finally resorting to dropping in on school--math and history and English class and all the teachers and everything they were saying and all the students. But nothing worked. Sleep wouldn't come and, my pulse throbbing wildly, I broke out in a cold clammy sweat.

Plunging my clammy hand under my mattress, I groped for and yanked out the two magazines, which promptly slipped out of my sweaty hands and splayed across the floor. In a flash, I scooped them up carried them surreptitiously back to my bed. Kneeling on the plush mattress, I flipped through the flashing brown and pink shiny pages, felt the warm gasping feeling coming on, the tingling in my feet, the buzzing head as my buttocks tightened and my beating arm grew tired with me feeling hot and dreamy. When it swept up and out of me, surging, everything went black and I fell backwards onto the bed, panting into sleep.

What woke me up the next morning was not a pounding in my head, but outside of it. Only after several minutes of blinking at the ceiling, did I realize that someone was hitting my bedroom door and shouting. I stood up, feeling raw and scraped out inside, and stepped towards the door.

"Hey, Del! Open up, assbite!"

Halfway to the door, I noticed I was nude, spun around and grabbed some shorts and a t-shirt from off the floor and slipped into them, wondering at the clear crusty stuff stuck to my inner thighs.

"Del! C'mon, let me in a sec!"

Just before opening the door, my peripheral vision caught a glint of the magazines still lying open on my bed. "*Shiiit!*" I whispered hoarsely to myself as I dashed over to my bed, closed the magazines and rammed them under the blankets, then I rushed back to the door, straightened my back and calmly swung it open.

"Took you long enough, dickhead," growled Kathy, stomping in past me. "Shut the door."

When I turned around, she was sitting on my bed. My heart jumped with the image of her finding what was stashed underneath the thin covers and I rapidly walked over to the bed and crawled onto the site where I thought they might be.

"Boy, do you look out of it."

Automatically, my hand rose to my hair. I tried to pat it down. "Whadayya want?" I said.

"Were you like stoned or somethin' last night?" asked Kathy, examining me through slitted eyes.

"No. Don't be stupid."

"Don't give me that crap. You were definitely trippin' on somethin'."

"Well, I had a beer. Dad said I could."

"You should have seen your eyes. That wasn't just beer. You were high." Kathy's gaze roved over my face, scanning.

"Was not. Look, what do you want anyways? Why are you in my room, just to give me the third degree?"

Kathy gave me this grown up look that told me that she knew I was lying but couldn't prove it. "OK," she said at last, "you were in the back yard late last night, right?"

I shrugged. "Think so."

"You were stoned alright."

"Shuddup."

"What a liar. Anyways, tell me what happened between dad and Al Wainwright."

"Whaddaya mean what happened?"

"There was some trouble between them."

"Trouble?"

"Yeah, a fight."

Vague images began floating up to the thinking, knowing part of my brain, images which I wasn't sure if I had dreamed them first and later they came true, or they had really happened and I dreamed them later on. "Let's see," I said. "I don't remember seein' a fight, but dad was mad at somethin' and then I remember seein' Al kinda twirlin' 'round and stuff and then he decided to lie down. I think he was probably drunk."

"You retard, Al wasn't dancin' or anythin'. There was a fight and daddy hit him. Boy, you were definitely trippin' on somethin', Del."

"Wasn't."

161

"Were, too. Anyway, there was a fight and mom got really pissed off."

"She's always pissed off. Lately anyways."

"No, I mean really pissed off this time." Kathy leaned in close to me, almost smiling. "Mom's split."

"Huh?

"Oh, c'mon moron, don't be so thick. Mom's gone. She's run off."

My mouth had dropped open. "What? Are you tryin' to fake me out?"

Kathy stared at me for an answer.

Unnerved, I said, "How do you know this?"

"Look, there was this fight last night, right? Between daddy and Al and mom I guess tried to stop it or somethin' and couldn't and then I guess she just couldn't stand it anymore. You know, dad and his rages and crazy trippin' all the time. Anyway, we--you know, Ernie and Rhonda and the others--we were all hangin' out in the driveway when out shoots mom and she like heads straight for the station wagon, gets in and zooms off. She never returned."

"Wow," I said numbly, not closing my mouth as my mind fumbled to comprehend.

"Some shit, huh?" said Kathy, almost smiling. "Who would have thought? I mean, I'm like the teenager here y'know. I'm the one who's supposed to run off, not my own mom. Talk about weird."

"Yeah," I said, and then, "Jeepers! What are we gonna do?"

Kathy laughed sardonically. "Good question. Nothin', I guess. Who ever heard of a mom runnin' away from home? We'll just have to hang out and see what happens."

"Yeah. What about the Mon--I mean, Mary Ellen? You think we oughta tell her?"

"No way. She'd only start cryin' her head off. Let's see what turns up. If it looks really serious, then we'll have to let her know. But let's just wait first."

"OK," I said weakly.

"Boy are you out of it, Del. What were you on last night anyways?"

"Nuthin'."

"Liar. OK, so don't tell me." Kathy stood up. "I'm takin' Smokey out for a ride. Dad's still asleep and I don't want to be around when he gets up. See you later."

"Yup," was all I could say.

"Jeez, what a stoner," said Kathy, shaking her head.

I wanted to tell her to shut up, but she was already gone. Then, my mind started grasping: gloved hands in a darkened room. Dull silence, a rasp of breath. Was it really true what Kathy had just told me? Could a mom just up and run off like that? Was that legal? Wasn't that just a TV thing that never happened in real life? The clawing fingers found no substance to cling to, the mind no explanations. Only a bewilderment, and on top of that a deep sinking in my stomach which produced a pounding pressure behind my eyes. Suddenly, I was lying on my stomach on my bed, crying.

I cried so hard for so long, a red, loose, runny-nosed baby cry, that at one point it wasn't even like crying any more but like throwing up, and I didn't know if I was crying for my mom anymore or for me or my dad or RFK or Davy's brother or just because I felt really tired and raw from whatever had happened to me last night. Then all at once the tears dried up and I was curled up in a tight ball, choking with snot running out of my nose and my stomach hurting. I sat up on the edge of the bed, blew my nose, then went down the hall to the bathroom where I blew my nose again, tried to pat down my wild and frizzed out hair, and washed my face. After staring blankly at myself in the mirror, I went outside to be with Cochise. It was too lonely in the bathroom.

On the way out, I came across the Monster with a Raggedy Anne doll hanging dead in her hand. "Hey Mary Ellen," I said, smiling thinly. I picked her up, squeezed her against my chest as if I hadn't seen her for a year and said, "Wanna come and play with the puppies?"

Mary Ellen kicked her legs. "OK, but lemmie go. I wanna walk."

"Alright." I set her down and tried to hold her hand, but she wouldn't let me; I don't know exactly why, but that kind of made me a little sad. Walking side-by-side, we went to the pole barn together.

I knew the puppies were not in the barn even before we had reached it. Everything was too still, too quiet. Duke walked up to me from where he had been sleeping in the shade under my dad's pickup, and licked my hand. "Here's Taffy," said Mary Ellen, bent over the doghouse. Peeking inside, I saw Taffy curled into a circle. She lifted her head, stared at us sullenly, and then closed her eyes and dropped her head again.

"Where are all the puppies, Del?"

"I don't know, Mary Ellen. Look under the trucks." Splitting up, we walked down opposite sides of each truck, got down on our knees and gazed into the murky shadow underneath, but found nothing. Suddenly, Mary Ellen gave out a little scream. "Del! There goes one!"

I ran over to her side just as a small black object came darting out from behind a wheel. At the sight of me, the pup halted and looked up into my face, growling in a low, menacing tone. His eyes were wet and had a wild, hateful look in them. Foam spewed out of his mouth. He snapped at me once, then rushed past, and raced up the large hill behind the barn.

Mary Ellen came up to me. "Did you see that? The puppy's sick."

"I don't think he's just sick, Mary Ellen," I swallowed hard, "I think he's got rabies or somethin'."

"I'm gonna tell daddy." Mary Ellen ran off to the house. After a second, I bolted after her.

Once in the kitchen, Mary Ellen headed towards my parents' bedroom. "Back yard," I yelled after her, knowing that no matter how hard he had worked or how much he had drunk the night before, my dad would not be inside at this time of day.

He was in the yard, standing with his back to us, hands in his pants' pockets, looking down at the dirt road down below, winding into the chaparral. In his loose white t-shirt, baggy pants and large, broad boots, my dad looked small and lost and swallowed up.

"Daddy!" shouted Mary Ellen, running up to him. "The puppies are sick!"

My dad spun around. His eyes looked old and tired, but still retained that underlining hardness. "What's that?"

I was standing in front of him now and he didn't appear so small anymore. "Somethin's wrong with the puppies. One of 'em gots foam comin' out of his mouth and they've all run away."

"They're all sick and got watery stuff in their eyes and noses and one of them did this to me "-- Mary Ellen growled --"and ran off up the big hill real fast."

A deep line furrowed between my dad's eyes. Something inside the pupils sparkled. "Now hold your horses for a second there. Del, tell me exactly what the hell's the matter with them pups."

"Don't know for sure. One is foamin' and actin' wild and he ran away into the bush."

"Where?"

"Big hill off from the pole barn."

"And the others? Was they foamin' too?"

Pictures from last night bubbled up into my consciousness. "Yeah, a couple of 'em. And last night I heard howlin' and stuff in the hills and I couldn't find the puppies anywhere."

My dad was still frowning. "Jesus," he said slowly, "at first I figured it was rabies, but it don't sound like it. Them poor little critters, I know what they gots. Distemper."

"What's that?" asked Mary Ellen.

"Puppy sickness," I said.

"Whatcha goin' to do, daddy? The puppies need our help."

My dad placed his large hand on Mary Ellen's head and stroked it. "Ain't nothin' we can do for 'em now, Mary Ellen. Once they gots it, that's it." Mary Ellen was craning her neck to look at my dad, with her mouth open in either disbelief or incomprehension. My dad rubbed her head again. "You run along and play now; I'll try and figure out a way to help 'em."

"Really?" smiled Mary Ellen.

"'I'll try my damnedest. You go on and play." We watched Mary Ellen run off to her room. When she was out of sight, my dad turned to me. "Del, distemper's a bad ass thing. We can't have no wild dogs runnin' round the joint, bitin' people. Hell, even Duke and Taffy and old Smokey wouldn't be safe neither. It's a hell of a thing."

"What do you mean?" I tried to swallow away the lump forming in my throat.

"They ain't no cure for them poor critters. They're sufferin', I'm sure. Go get the .22 and some shells and put your boots on. Meet me out front."

Numb and unthinking, I went first to my room and slipped on my boots, then to my parents' bedroom to get the .22 from out of the closet and a box of shells from my dad's sock drawer. I rejoined him in the driveway. He was holding a burlap sack and frowning again. Taking the rifle from my hands, he gave me the sack and I passed him the box of shells. He snapped the clip out of the .22, pressed in eight brass-jacketed shells and clicked it back into place. Working the bolt, he slid a shell into the chamber, set the safety catch and slung the rifle over one shoulder. "Let's go," he said.

As we passed the barn, Duke trotted out at us then stopped and lifted his nose at the rifle. Instantly, he lowered his head, pulled his tail tight between his legs and turned right around and slunk away.

"Duke sure is gun-shy," I said.

"Yeah. So am I," said my dad. "I hate the damn things."

We were climbing uphill now, the powdered earth rising up in yellow-brown clouds as our boots sank into it. It was hot, the air still and slightly oppressive. I sneezed from the dust and wiped my hand on my jeans leg. Once we reached the top of the hill, we set out along a path cutting through the chaparral. My dad coughed, then spat off to one side. He cleared his throat.

"You know your mom's took off." From the way he said it, I wasn't sure if it was a question or a statement.

"Huh?" I said and then added with awkwardness, "Oh, yeah. Kathy told me this mornin'."

Our boots rose and fell on the soft sand of the path. A twig snapped under my heel.

"Yup," said my dad, "Late last night. Guess she's sore at me or somethin'. Christ, I don't know." He spat again, sudden dark staining the dry earth. I didn't know what to say, so said nothing. I don't know why, but I felt sort of stiff and embarrassed.

We trudged on through the dust and the brittle bush, eyes scanning ahead of us and cutting from side to side, trying to penetrate the snarled undergrowth. Suddenly in front of us there arose a howl followed by two plaintive baying sounds. My dad lifted the rifle from his shoulder and held it in both hands, barrel pointed to the ground. A metallic click told me that he had released the safety. Tensely, we moved along the trail through the chaparral, pungent with the aroma of resin. Our feet pressed silently into the dusty earth. Holding my breath, my heart began pounding so violently I was sure my dad could hear it; if he did, he didn't show it. Instead, his small, granite eyes were fixed ahead of him, his nostrils almost flaring from the scent of something. *Whoomp, whoomp, whoomp!* boomed my heart.

A black blur dashed out of the bush to the right of us and stopped, an angry ball of white foam and wet flashing eyes. Crouching, my dad raised the rifle, sucked in a breath and the chaparral exploded. Birds screamed and fluttered, I jerked backwards and a small black object lay flat and still on the ground. Instantly, the bush was deathly quiet again, and the only sound was that of the ringing in my ears.

We stepped up to the tiny crumpled thing lying in front of us. I could see no blood.

"Hand me them gloves in the sack, Del," said my dad quietly. "Poor little bastard," he mumbled, handing me the rifle and putting on the leather gloves. Bending down, he grasped the dead pup by the hind legs and lifted the flaccid, rubbery body up into the sack. Dark and syrup thick, a small stream of blood trickled onto the dry ground. I gave the rifle back to my dad and he passed me the sack, which was noticeably weighted now.

"Goddamn it, I hate shit like this," said my dad, blinking at the drops of blood in the dirt. We were silent for a moment, then he stirred, saying, "Well, let's get on with it. The others gotta be around here somewheres close."

The hunt continued. The rifle cracked again after fifteen minutes, and shortly after that we came across two more in a yellow grassy area. One of these was Frank, Mary Ellen's dog. I felt sick when my dad dropped him heavily into the sack. We did the work silently, with grim, stricken faces. Another, black with white feet, lay panting in the shade of the bush. The rifle was raised and slowly brought down. The dark stain at the bottom the sack widened.

"How many's that?" my dad asked me. Sweating and breathing hard, I set the sack down. It weighed a ton now.

"Five," I said, suddenly realizing with a start what that meant. My dead heart started throbbing again and the nausea rose in my throat.

"That makes one more, then we can quit this god dammed job," said my dad.

I nodded without saying a word. There was one more puppy left.

We hung around an open area, bristling with deer-trampled dried grass. We had heard a growling bark coming from this area, and knew the last pup was nearby. I had laid the burlap sack under a bush, and was crunching through the grass, searching about five feet away from where my dad walked, eyes roving. Then I came to an abrupt stop. "Dad," I said in a normal voice that hid the sob caught in my throat. "Over here." I heard my dad's heavy step and felt, rather than saw, him standing next to me.

"Hell, Del," he said, "that's your pup, ain't it?"

"Yeah," I whispered, not taking my eyes off of Cochise. He sat on his haunches at the edge of the bush, mouth open. He didn't have that wild, mad look in his eyes that the others had, but they were moist and you could see the flecks of foam at the corners of his mouth.

"You wanna do it?" My dad offered me the .22.

I shook my head. "Can't," I tried to say but the word got stuck in my throat. I closed my eyes and waited, fingers twitching. Hours crawled by. Beyond the deep bass of my pounding heart, I heard a lizard moving through the dried grass. The leaves of a nearby tree rustled slightly. Somewhere far away a bird was singing. Then a violent roar blasted my mind into emptiness. For several minutes the rifle's report echoed in my head and I felt shivery cold and clammy and salt burned my eyes. My chest heaved dry voiceless sobs that hurt but would not come all the way out of my body, then suddenly sank down into me and melted away. It was all over.

Retracing our footsteps along the trail, my dad and I each held a corner of the sack because it was so heavy. It swung between us, a few red drops tearing out from the wet bottom and plopping silently onto the path. Red jewels lay between the oblong lattice impressions of our boot soles. We carried the puppies down the big hill and out behind the pole barn where I left the sack with my dad and went to the barn to get a shovel. Under the yellow sun, my dad watched, wiping the sleek beads of sweat from his forehead, as I dug a broad and deep hole into the hard, crusty earth. When it was deep enough, we laid the dripping sack with flies now buzzing around and clinging to it into the hole, and I covered it with dirt. My back hurt and my hands felt raw from the wooden shovel handle. When the hole was filled and my dad had stomped on it to pack down the earth I rolled a large stone on top of it to mark the spot forever, and then we both turned away and, unspeaking, returned to the house. I was tired, and my head hung down.

Mary Ellen was waiting for us at the kitchen door. She must have spotted us as we came down the hill with the sack swaying between us.

"What happened Del?" she demanded as I approached.

"Nuthin'."

Mary Ellen's face had a hard, grown up look to it. "I heard the gun go bang. What did you do?"

"Leave me alone, OK?"

"I counted 'em, Del. It went bang six times."

"Oh, Mary Ellen we had to, OK? It was the only way. Oh, please just shut up and leave me alone."

Mary Ellen's face turned scarlet and then crumpled up on itself as she burst into tears. "I hate you!" she sobbed. "I hate you all!" And she turned and ran inside.

My dad glanced over at me and said, "She'll get over it. Little kids is like that."

"Yeah," I nodded, then went into my bedroom, closed the door and lay down on my bed with an arm across my eyes. I was so tired, too tired to think. Too tired to cry. In a few moments, I had drifted off into sleep.

I awoke with a frightened gasp and clung to the sides of the bed to keep from falling. Mouth open, my face pointing up to the ceiling, my eyes traveled in my unmoving head, eyes crawling over the walls and pictures, the tiny airplanes and the dusty books, everything shrouded in gray shadow. I stood up, feeling dizzy, and stumbled into the hall. Shadow dripped off of every wall, spreading in slow oozing pools across the floor. The air was stale and dead and heavy and I began to panic, suddenly feeling as if I couldn't breathe. With fumbling fingers, I opened the door to the yard, and stepped out into late summer.

"There you are, Del," said a voice to one side of me. Startled, I looked up. "I been callin' you for the longest. Ain't you heard me?"

asked my dad. His voice sounded fuzzy, unclear.

"No. I was sleepin'."

"Sleepin'! Shit, still broad daylight. Get yer ass over here and water these plants. This heat's knocked the god dammed hell out of 'em." The words were all slurred.

Passing near my dad on the way to the hose, I saw a bottle of gin on the small wooden table next to him, only one-third full. Next to this was a bottle of tonic water, a soup bowl filled with ice, a sliced lemon and my dad's open pocketknife. When he raised his glass to drink, the ice inside chimed musically.

"Hotter, hotter'n hell, boy. That's for damn sure."

I picked up the hose, kinked it to block the water from gushing out over the bricks, and turned the tap on.

"Hit them daisies first. Thems the one's as needs it."

Placing my thumb over the nozzle, I let a soft cascade of water glide over the thirsty, half-wilted flowers.

"Hotter'n a sonfabitch, boy." Ice sang against the sides of the glass. "Water 'em good, Del. Atta boy. You're alright, you're alright. That was a hell of thing we done today, you know that? Sonofabitch. But we hadda do it. Hadda be done so we done it, hey boy? Hell yes." I could hear more gin and the fizz of tonic water being poured into my dad's glass behind me. I moved over to water the ferns. "Jesus H. Christ, what a job we done. Them poor pups. Shit like that just tears your heart out. You wanna beer or a gin, Del, you just go ahead and fix yourself one. You done earned it today for what we done. Hell yes, you just go ahead, boy. Sonofabitch. What a world. I didn't mean to hit that bastard like that, but he pushed on me. Sonofabitch pushed on me and ain't nobody can do that. Can't get away with that. What the hell? That's just the way I get sometimes is all, you listening to me?" My dad's voice rose a little and I turned, somewhat frightened, to see what he wanted. But he wasn't really talking to me, so I continued to water. "I just see red, is all, so don't be pushin' on me unless'n you mean somethin' by it. Christ, so she had to run off like that. Hell, I only hit 'im once and that's 'cause he pushed on me. Is that any god dammed reason to up and run off? That's what I'm askin'. Is that any damn reason?" My dad's tone, the slurred words with a choked, cut off

170

quality to them, was frightening me. I wasn't sure if he was about to pass out from drink, break down into tears or jump up and hit me. So I just stood there, frozen, listening, waiting, splashing water out over everything before me, including my own feet. The water hit the ground with a *slap!*

"What a fucked up world. Jesus H. Christ, I don't know what the hell's happenin' anymore. Everythin's goin' to hell. Long hair dope head kids in the streets, riots and shit, Kennedy shot. Hell, Kathy don't even mind her own mom and dad and Mary Ellen's got her face stuck in the boob tube all the time and Del and shit..." My body tightened at the mention of my name, but the drawled drunken monologue passed me by "...all breakin' down, you hear me? This ain't where I growed up. It weren't like this before, twenty-five years ago. Things was simpler back then, better. Now everythin's shot to hell. This country's back-broke. Somethin's gone all screwy and wrong." I heard my dad suck in a long drink. "Christ," and then, after a pause, "Sarah. You can't do that. You'll be back alright, and it'll be alright, you just wait an' see, boy. Ain't right no how anyways, I oughta...aw, the hell with it. It's all shot to hell...I only hit the bastard once..."

My dad's voice trailed away and I pinched off the water and slowly turned around. His chin was resting on his chest, and one arm hung straight down, an empty glass held in his big paw. Before I could react, the glass slipped out and shattered on the brick floor. I cringed, but my dad didn't even stir. Quietly, I tipped-toed to the tap and twisted it off, holding my breath each time it squeaked, then dropped the hose and ran to my bedroom, leaving the snoring, huge form of my dad sunken in the wicker chair, as night enveloped him in its long, black arms.

14

It's pretty weird when you don't have a mom. The house feels colder, even in the summertime. The air is empty of those special mom-noises of clattering pots and pans, a whistling kettle, her humming a favorite song, the squeak and *pfumpf* of oven and refrigerator doors closing and, some time around late afternoon, those certain, weary sighs after the housework's done and the kids are all outside and your mom flops on the couch with a book or magazine and bows her head to vanish from this world for a few precious stolen minutes until your dad comes home.

You miss the mom-smells as well, of frying bacon and eggs or roasting chicken, the wholesome, happy aroma of baked potatoes and bread, or perhaps a wispy hint of perfume lingering in the rooms which she passes through, or the hard, chemical scents of tile cleaner and powdered soap or a whiff of just-vacuumed rug swirling in the living room air. Smells and sounds of life and activity. Of a presence, and a living warmth. Remove that and you've taken away an essential essence that transforms a mere structure of brick and wood and stone into a home.

The two days after by mom had left and the shooting of the puppies were little more than a hazy blur to me, an empty, gloomy time. I had no appetite, which was probably for the better because the runny eggs, burnt toast and canned beans my dad called dinner would not have stayed for very long in my stomach. Listlessly, I hung around in my room, flipping with no interest through the girlie magazines and my comics, or sat numbly in the living room, staring with unfocused eyes and opened mouth at the smiling, screaming people who lived inside the electric blue box with the fake wood paneling for sides. I went for a long walk once, with good ole Duke at my side, and stopped by the puppies' graves to drop a wild flower on top of the mound. Duke seemed to sense what was buried underneath this new and unnatural heap of earth, and he stayed several yards away from it as I lingered, mumbling ineffectual and unheard goodbyes.

I would have run off to be with Ronni if I could have, but that was out of the question. My dad was at work all day long, and Kathy out with her friends: if she missed either our mom or the puppies, she didn't show it. So that left me to watch over the Monster. I think my mom's not being there was quite agreeable to her because I was an unqualified and lax ersatz parent. Mary Ellen could watch TV whenever she wanted, didn't have to bath or comb her unruly hair, could munch on cookies and potato chips instead of fruit and never had to clean her room. For all she knew and for all we told her, our mom was out shopping or visiting friends or her sister in L.A. She would return, the Monster knew intrinsically, even as she knew, or rather felt, that the puppies were unreturning. She had seen my dad with the .22. He and I had gone away in the hills wearing boots and Duke had not followed. There had been bangs like the bangs on TV and then a stillness in the air which had stopped cold all animal and human sounds and the likes of which had never been experienced on our ranch before. The Monster had witnessed all this. Who knows, maybe my dad and I had had the smell of killing and death on us when we returned that day in the late afternoon, tense and unsmiling and carrying a gun and a dripping sack and wearing our boots. Perhaps the Monster had sensed this in an unspoken way and had had a gut feeling that the puppies were gone and would not be coming back, forever. But whatever she felt or knew, neither one of us ever spoke about the puppies again, nor what had really happened in the hills.

In the morning of the second day of my mom's leaving, I was awoken my a ringing in my head that when I opened my eyes became a ringing in the hallway that would not stop. After a bleary waking-up second, I sprang out of bed and rushed out into the hall to the phone.

"Hello?"

"Del? This is mom."

Startled, I remained speechless.

"What took you so long to answer the phone? Is everything OK?"

"Ye-Yes.." Rapidly, my brain emerged from its sleep-daze. "Mom, you comin' home?"

"How's Mary Ellen? Is she alright?" It was strange to talk to my mom on the phone. Her voice sounded different, like she was speaking into an empty tin can. "Is Kathy around?"

"Everyone's fine, mom," I said. "When are you gonna come home?"

"Del, is your father there?"

"No. He's at work."

"Good," she sighed loudly. "Look, I'm coming over right now."

"Great!"

"But not for good, Del." Tiny knives stabbed into my stomach. "I have to pick up a few things. And I want to get Mary Ellen. She'll stay with me here for awhile, Del. Del?"

"Yes?" I said quietly.

"Please get Mary Ellen ready for me. Dressed and with shoes on, OK? Put her toothbrush and her favorite toys in a bag for me. I'll be right over."

"Mom," it was difficult to talk through a tightening throat. "Why aren'tcha gonna come home and stay?"

Another sigh. "Oh, Del, please understand. Try to understand me, my situation." She stopped and I could hear her breathing into the phone. "Look, I'm coming right over and I'll try to explain things to you, alright? It's so awkward on the phone like this. I'll be right there. I love you. Bye."

"Bye," I said, just as it all swelled up and I started to cry. "I love you mom."

Deep, measured breaths and splashing cold water on my face helped to stop the crying. I found Mary Ellen in her bedroom, playing with her Barbies. I told her to go brush her hair and put her shoes on and that mom was coming and they were going to take a ride together. "And take your favorite Barbie and your toothbrush."

"Why do I gotta take my toothbrush for if we're goin' drivin'?" asked Mary Ellen.

"'Cause you might stop somewhere and eat ice cream. Now hurry up, mom'll be here in a sec."

Mary Ellen pulled on her socks and shoes and I tried to help her comb her snarled hair. Then she went into the bathroom and came out carrying two toothbrushes. "Here," she said, holding mine up to me.

"What's that for?"

"If I gotta brush my teeth, you gotta, too."

"I'm not goin', Mary Ellen. Just you and mom."

"Why ain'tcha comin'?"

"'Aren't you'."

"Ain'tcha comin' too, Del?" The way Mary Ellen was looking up at me, with big eyes and an open mouth, almost started me crying again.

"No. Just you and mom for now."

"Why come?"

"'Cause I got things to do. I gotta...mom says I gotta pull weeds."

"Oh," nodded Mary Ellen. "That stinks."

"Yeah," I said, "you lucked out."

A moment later, Duke called to us that a car was moving up the dirt road. It was my mom's red station wagon. We met her in the driveway. The sight of her getting out of the car, with that one lock of hair hanging over her eyes and wearing a warm, sad smile, gave me a hollow feeling in my chest and my head and eyes started to throb.

"Mommy!" screamed Mary Ellen, running to my mom, who picked her up and held her against her chest with both arms. My mom closed her eyes and pressed her face into Mary Ellen's hair. Setting her down, my mom came up to me and gave me a big hug and kissed me on the forehead. My eyes were shut tight to keep the tears back, and I drank in her special mom-smell of perfume and creams and freshness. "Del," was all she said, her voice sounding tight. Letting go of me, she turned to Mary Ellen. "All set? Got your toothbrush?"

"Oops, I forgot," said Mary Ellen. "It's on my bed."

"Well, run along and get it. Del and I will be in my bedroom."

In the bedroom, my mom got a small leather bag out of the closet, and put a few articles of clothing inside. From off the night table near her side of the bed, she took three paperback books and placed them in the bag as well. Then she sat on the edge of the bed and looked around the bedroom, as if she'd never seen it before or had been away for a long time.

"Mom," I said. "Stay."

"I can't, Del. At least not right now. I need to get away, to take a break. I think you're old enough to know the reason why."

"I don't understand. We're a family. Things aren't suppose to work this way in a family."

"Del, I know it's difficult, but you have to understand. I'm tired, and I need a break. Your father is such a hard, unreasonable man. I can't take it anymore."

"But the kids can all help you." My body was trembling with the fight to keep back the tears, but also with an inarticulate rage that made me want to smash my fist into the wall.

"Right now, nobody can help me but myself. Del, look around you. The world is changing. Can't you feel it, like there's is something new and different dawning? Your father can't keep on acting the way he does and expect me--and you kids--to mutely take it. It's my life too, you know."

"Can't you just sit down and talk to him or somethin'"

"I will, but first I'm taking a little break to think things out for myself. I'll talk when I'm good and ready. Besides, if I tried it now he'd only fly into one of his rages and we'd be right back where we are now."

Mary Ellen burst into the room, holding a tin sand pail in her hand, filled with toys. She gripped her toothbrush in the other. "Ready!" Her eyes sparkled with the light of adventure. "You don't get any ice cream, Del."

"I don't want one," I said under my breath. I bit into my lower lip, trying hard not to cry. My mom stood up. Her eyes were glassy.

"Well, Del," she said but that's all I heard because I was running full speed out of the house, into the summer's yellow blinding light, up past the pole barn with its silent brooding tucks and sleeping dogs, uphill into the choking dust and the thin scratchy arms of the chaparral.

Eyes on fire, lungs straining hard to draw in the thick air, I ran along a sandy path, slowing gradually to a rapid walk as the sun pressed against my chest and head like a heavy, molten hand. My pace slowed further and I walked with my hands on my hips, trying to catch my breath. With the heat and all the exertion the crying feeling slunk back down into the dark shafts tunneled into my chest and stomach from where it had arisen. Walking was always my medicine. I walked on.

The low, sloping hill leading down to Ritchie Lane's house was covered with the tall stalks of yellow grass which snapped and cracked as I moved through them. As I neared the house, the front door opened and a figure ran out towards me. Almost involuntarily I began smiling, an odd feeling because the skin on my face felt tightly stretched and dry. I waved.

"Del!" yelled Ronni, waving enthusiastically back.

I motioned for her to stay where she was, and ran, until we stood face-to-face, me sweating and smiling, she looking deep into my eyes and grinning. Then we hugged and I kissed her on her cheek and behind her ear, breathing in the special smell of her hair. "Oh, Del," she whispered. "I wanted you to come so bad."

Hand-in-hand, we turned towards the house. "Del, I was afraid you were not going to come. It's been such a long time since you were last here and I couldn't call because we don't have a phone."

"Yeah, well, somethin' happened back at my house."

"What do you mean? Is something wrong?"

"Oh, no. It's just that my dad freaked out, the puppies are dead and my mom's run away from home is all."

"Don't joke, Del."

"I'm not," I said grimly. "I wish I was though."

"What are you talking about?" asked Ronni, as we walked under the shade of a large oak tree near the house. Sitting down with our sides pressed against each other, our backs to the tree and my hand in hers, I told all that had happened since the night of my dad's party. When I had finished, I felt drained, weak in my body and exhausted in my mind.

"Oh, Del," said Ronni, stroking my cheek, "I'm probably the only

177

person you know who can say 'I understand,' and really mean it."

"You definitely are."

Ronni gave me a hug and squeezed my hand. "It's all so terrible, but I'm glad you're here. I was so afraid you wouldn't come back."

"Don't be a moron. You know I'd always come to see you and your sister and Ritchie."

"No," said Ronni, with a different tone in her voice. "I know that. I know you wouldn't forget about me or anything. It's just that my momma wrote a few days ago."

"Good. What did she say?"

"Well, it's not so good, Del. She's doing kind of badly. She's sick and all and you know my screwed up family, there's nobody there who can take care of her."

"Why doesn't she go to a doctor?"

"Can't afford it. So," said Ronni, laying her head on my shoulder. "It looks like I'll be going back to Detroit sooner than I thought."

"What?" I said, my body tightening.

"Don't be mad, Del. I have to go."

"You can't go."

"I have to. It's my momma. She needs me."

"But it's not fair. The summer's not even over yet." Inside me was panic, everything sinking and dropping rapidly away as an empty bottomless feeling opened up in my chest. Simultaneously, my face buzzed with heat and I clenched my hand into a fist. "I'm goin' with you."

"You can't, Del. It's not possible."

"I'll run away, I'll steal some money from my dad and go back with you."

"Don't be silly."

"I'm not. I totally mean it."

"You couldn't steal that much money anyway, Del. Besides, you wouldn't like it in Detroit."

"I'd like it if you were there."

"No you wouldn't," said Ronni and I could feel the muscles in her back growing tense. "It's not like here. It's a grown-up place. In Detroit, everybody's a big person. There aren't any children."

"I'm not a kid anymore. That's what everyone's been tellin' me lately. I could be a grown-up, too."

"No you couldn't, not there. You can just pop up in Detroit and be one. It has to be something you grew up in, there's this look on people's faces there, Del, a frowning, hard look that you just don't have. Maybe I have it, I don't know. Probably, because everybody in my neighborhood has it." Ronni looked up at me, her eyes red and moist. "Del, you don't have that look. They'd see that right away and you wouldn't have a chance." She turned her eyes away from me.

"We could run away somewhere nice together," I said as my stomach sank and my eyes began hurting.

"You're talking stupid now and you know it. I'm just glad you came."

"When are you leavin'?"

"Real soon. Too soon. Ritchie and Bernadine are buying my plane ticket right now. Probably tomorrow or the next day."

"Is Morn--I mean your sister goin', too?

"No," said Roni. "She's staying. She says she'll never go back for nobody no how. She hates it back there."

"I hate it, too."

"Me, too."

"Then stay."

"Oh, I can't, get it?" Ronni suddenly snapped. "School'll be starting up and my momma needs me." Then her voice softened. "Besides, I'll be back."

"No you won't," I said quietly, my head suddenly flooded with a thousand sad summer images. "People don't come back anymore."

"I'll be back, Del. I promise."

"No you won't," I said. My voice was hoarse, and suddenly I was crying big, fat stinging tears. "No you won't, I know you won't."

Ronni was crying now as well. "Don't say that Del. Don't talk that way."

I felt spent, cold inside, devoid of energy. The trauma of tears, the summer's relentless, hammering sun, my mom and the long walk over here and the still, lifeless air: it all exhausted me and I felt there were no more words to say, nothing that could be said. I heaved for breath.

I stood up and Ronni grabbed my arm.

"Don't go, Del. Stay here with me for a while longer."

"No. I'm tired. I wanna go home." I was crying fresh tears again. "Bye," I choked, "try and not forget me, OK?"

"I'll be back, Del. I promise I'll be back."

The voice was behind me, growing smaller, behind the gasped sobs jerking from my chest, behind the hill I was climbing up as fast as my weak legs could carry me. Up ahead, beyond the crest of the hill and floating above there was only the magnificent, swirling sun, a winding path of sand, spiny bushes with blue arms outstretched towards me, some pointing out past the haze of chaparral, showing me the shimmering silent trail leading home.

15

Home, and I was dazed and reeling. Exhausted, I crawled into my room, lay on my bed and curled into a tight protective cocoon with drawn up knees and hunched back armoring the soft, damageable underbelly and the organs throbbing inside. Safe, I closed my eyes. It was time to sleep now. Sleep, the healing. You never cry in your sleep, and in sleep the cuts and slashes of the waking time are soothed and repaired; sheer and delicate threads suture the broken parts back together again without hurt, without recognition. Sleep makes it all possible, especially a dreamless one. Not dreaming is important because if you don't dream, maybe you can forget; the healing is in the forgetting is in the sleep. Only then can you begin to gather the lost pieces. Asleep, I drifted away.

Early morning of a quiet summer's day and I got up once again to eat alone at the kitchen table. My dad was at work, my mom and Mary Ellen still gone, Kathy out somewhere. The spoon in my hand clinked loud and harsh against the china bowl. It was a lonely sound and I didn't like it so I ate quickly. But while eating, I decided what to do.

When I had finished, I took a brick of cheddar cheese out of the refrigerator, sliced wedges off of it and made two sandwiches with mayonnaise, sweet brown mustard, diced green onions and sliced tomato on nutty brown bread. From the fruit bowl I grabbed an orange and a red apple. Returning to my room, I got my U.S. army canteen from out of the closet and pulled on my boots. I put the sandwiches and fruit into my army surplus backpack and went outside, stopping at a tap to fill the canteen. Cold water trickled over my fingers and felt good.

I twisted the tap closed, stood up, twined my arms through the backpack's shoulder straps and attached the canteen to my pants' belt loops. The day was bright, clear, fresh, the boiling mornings of high summer now gone, a tinge of autumn just making itself felt by a subtle change of color in the sky, the way shadows lingered in cool pools at the side of the house and a certain smell in the air. I called for Duke and, smiling, he came bounding up at me from deep inside the pole barn.

Together we set out, crossing the wooden fence bordering the driveway, and crunching through the tall, dead yellow grass pasture leading to the horse barn. The grass glimmered golden in the buttery bars of the early morning sun. Nearing the barn, I came across a large stone that looked vaguely familiar to me and, pausing to gaze at it, I remembered. I sank down to my knees and turned the rock over. Duke stuck his nose down into the depression the rock had made and I pushed him away. In the soft, rich earth laid the delicate white bones of the lizard that Davy and I had buried long ago. I had planned to preserve the skeleton and keep it as some sort of curiosity or specimen for biology class at school. But gazing down at the remains, picked clean by ants and worms, I suddenly decided that the old lizard deserved better than that. Why stick him in a shoebox at home or into some cold jar in the lab at school? That didn't seem right somehow so, using a stick, I dug out a hole in the ground, cupped my hand into the earth underneath the lizard so as not to disturb the dignity of the fragile skeleton, and carefully placed him at the bottom of his grave. I looked at him lying there for a long minute. Then I pushed dirt on top, stomped on it with the heel of my boot to pack it down firmly, and rolled the stone back over it. Now he could sleep undisturbed.

Duke and I crossed through the corral, Smokey watching us out of the sides of his head and lifting his nose to snort. We crawled under the wooden fence at the far end of the corral, and struck out uphill along a deer trail, tattooed with fresh tracks. We moved on at an easy pace, pausing to watch cottontails nibbling in the undergrowth, trying to stalk invisible flocks of quail which we could hear bickering all around us but could never locate, or staring upwards at the meandering paths of hawks and buzzards soaring high overhead.

The morning burned off fast and the growing warmth and the hiking made me feel weak. I halted under a large tree with a flattened, sandy area around its base, slipped off the backpack, which was dark from sweat, and sat down with my back up against the good, solid firmness of the tree trunk. The water in my canteen was lukewarm, but it still tasted fine and I drank as I watched Duke drop his head low to the ground, sniffing, and trot off into the bush. Then I ate one of the cheese and tomato sandwiches and reached into the backpack to take out the orange, its sharp, acidic aroma bursting into the air as I sank my thumbnail into the rippled peel. This tangy orange smell in the hot air, mingling with the sweet scent of the dry grass and the rich aroma of crusty earth, was summer to me, but what a summer this one had been. I blinked and let out a sigh. This summer had been a real punch in the gut, a hard kick in the ass. It was nearly over, but still going strong. From overseas had come news of street fighting in Czechoslovakia and here at home in Chicago. Vietnam was in ruins. All over the planet cities were burning. Everywhere--on the TV, in newspapers and magazines--there were cutout gray spaces where there once had been women and men and children. They were Gone People now, a long, thin trail of vaporous forms starting at some foggy point in the distance and dropping into the haze-obscured horizon. They weren't ever coming back again. A hell of a summer, I could almost hear my dad saying. A hell of a time. Why was it that everything moved so fast and yet so painfully slow, a long, hard process that would never end?

But the summer would end. It always ended. The new school year would soon be starting, as it always had started, and with it new Teachers and Bullies and Fat Kids and the Girl with a Gap in Her Front Teeth and the Shy Kid who wouldn't play dodge ball with the others and so would get mercilessly teased. They'd all be there again. The school would grind on just as the nation would go on, inexorably. Only limping now. A hell of a summer. A hell of a time. Maybe people would even laugh again. The people would laugh but they'd probably never be happy again. That was the difference. In this summer everyone had been touched, and everyone had died a little. There were things gone that were never going to come back, ever. Christ, I could hear my dad grumbling to himself, a hell of a time.

If this was growing up, I didn't want it. I'd rip the hairs out of my chin, eat badly to keep myself stunted and small, flunk out of school-- anything to hang on to that which was leaving. I'd do almost anything at all.

A loud rustling and Duke crashed out of the bush, a twig clinging to the matted fur of his shoulder. He walked briskly up and sat right down in front of me, sticking his nose in my face, licking at the salt streams draining my eyes. His tongue, wet and firm, stroked my aching eyes until I smiled. Patting him on the head, I stood up, slipped on my backpack, clipped the canteen onto my belt loops, and set off with him along the trail, a slight breeze with crisp tinges of early autumn in it shaking the tops of the chaparral, the air warm but moving, a grand and blistering sun melting across my shoulders.

Up ahead on the trail, Duke suddenly stood still, his neck twisted as he looked back at me with a cocked head, a quizzical expression on his face, probably wondering why I had stopped. But a thought had just hit me, a serious, straight-forward, no nonsense grown-up thought: for the first time that I could remember--perhaps for the first time in my life--I found myself wishing for something that I had never wished for before.

That the summer would end.

ABOUT THE AUTHOR

Raised on a ranch in the chaparral-covered hills of Central California, O'Brien Browne writes fiction, blogs and feature articles on history, personal development and culture. He is a *Huffington Post* blogger and a Contributing Editor at *The Quarterly Journal of Military History.* He has lived internationally with a variety of occupations. Browne holds degrees from U.C. Berkeley and New York University, and runs *Open Minds Open Markets*, a global people and business development organization.

Purchase other Black Rose Writing titles at www.blackrosewriting.com/books

and use promo code PRINT to receive a 20% discount.

CPSIA information can be obtained at www.ICGtesting.com
Printed in the USA
LVOW05s0312150115

422902LV00034B/1530/P